I0713600

EDGE OF REALITY

STRINGS & THINGS DARK ENERGY
TEMPORAL ENIGMAS

THOMAS BOUR

EDGE OF REALITY:
STRINGS & THINGS DARK ENERGY TEMPORAL ENIGMAS

This book is written to provide information and motivation to readers. Its purpose is not to render any type of psychological, legal, or professional advice of any kind. The content is the sole opinion and expression of the author, and not necessarily that of the publisher.

Copyright © 2019 by Thomas Bour

Printed in the United States of America.

ISBN   978-1-949746-50-1   (Paperback)
ISBN   978-1-949746-51-8   (Digital)

Lettra Press books may be ordered through booksellers or by contacting:

Lettra Press LLC
18229 E 52nd Ave.
Denver City, CO 80249
1 303 586 1431 | info@lettrapress.com
www.lettrapress.com

Table of Contents

Thomas Bour is a scientifically curious individual within the framework of humanity, writing words on pages for constructive entertainment, and conscious enlightenment. The act of observation leads individuals on the life journey into his string theory discussion, rooted within the multi-dimensional aspects of reality. Individuals interact within reality's stage as conscious life abounds on earth. The author entangles his string theories multi-dimensional reality into ordinary life, allowing non-scientific individuals to enjoy its wonderous aspects into which they are immersed. A simplistic discussion into a thought provoking and amazing perspective on a question rooted deep within humanity. When science and spirituality merge into a single aspect of reality to which the mind is content not to debate discrepancies of nuance. Read and enjoy the "Edge of reality."

Edge of Reality

by Thomas Bour

This book contains a discussion with a new perspective on the old Sting Theory problems; with respect to where are all of those extra dimensions, we need to make the theory work mathematically are hiding. It has been said by many scientists, that we may need to look at the String Theory problem with a fresh perspective, or find new ways of thinking to resolve it challenges. Let have a little fun with open minds, and a new way of looking into reality with our imaginations turned on, as we discuss possible new solutions to resolving the String Theory challenges. This discussion will provoke a new way of thinking about the reality in which we find ourselves immersed within.

Exercising the mind, is one way to look into things that are out of reach of direct experimentation. Einstein utilized the thought experiments to revolutionize modern physics, by means of imagination, insight and logic. This discussion proceeds in language which most anyone can follow, regardless of background. This is an intuitive discussion, with respect to known and accepted foundational science principles, focused on solving the string theory challenges, with new ways of thinking about said challenges.

Introduction

The goal of science is to be able to explain reality in a simple matter of fact statement, that most individuals can understand and accept as plausible. Over the years science has made great progress towards achieving its ultimate goal. There have been numerous breakthroughs, and even more plausible theories as to how everything works in reality. Many of the scientific theories deal with topics that are on the edge of human understanding and experimental possibilities. There yet remain many questions to the nature of reality, especially in the field of physics.

Questions such as, where did all of the matter in the big bang explosion come from. It has been speculated that it was created from energy, which was the result of the big bang explosion fourteen billion years ago. It was speculated! Creationist maintain that god created the universe, by divine nature. It was speculated.

Speculation will be at the heart of this extended discussion which will address string theory, dark energy, and dark matter. We will also discuss where all the matter in the universe may have actually came from. Our discussions will stray into the outer edge of our universe, and phenomena which may be causing some of the above-mentioned phenomena. We will be speculating on the edge of reality, the place where science and reason hope to meet up in a plausible mannerism.

The edge of reality discussion will attempt to put all of the science, and astrophysics questions in a plausible, and unified state of being. If this is possible and reality can be explained in a single format, (unified field theory) we might find ourselves a little bit closer to understanding the manner in which reality is assembled, and functions around all of us. In order to assemble a unified field theory, or more precisely, a set of unified field theories, we will have to open our minds to new ways of thinking. We can achieve this goal with new perspectives on how reality has been assembled for our observational experiences.

This discussion will break reality down into its foundational building block components. The next phase of the discussion will be to convince the reader of the perspective accuracy in which the discussion is proceeding. The discussion will then provide examples of how the dimensional parameters apply to reality with respect to string theory parameters and requirements mathematically, in laymen terms. There will be no complex mathematics in this discussion, those will be left to the individual professional mathematicians capable of such an undertaking. Finally, the discussion will enter into a proof statement of how all of the discussion material fits into the string theory model, with a fun little rocket ship ride analogy to pull it together.

Being able to see the forest for the trees, may be the approach which aids in our quest to redefine reality, in the parameteristic boundaries, that an actual string theory allows mathematically.

Remember looking at one of those squiggly lines looking, Magic Eye pictures. The ones that you have to distort your visual focus, in order to actually see the hidden picture contained on the page. The Magic Eye pictures do not look anything at all like the pictures they contain, until the observer attains the correct perspective visual focus. A new way of looking at something, is required to realize the intended observation of the magic eye artwork designs.

With open minds, and a new mental perspective focus at the ready, we can all enjoy the mental ride that the "Edge of reality" will provide. Scientific speculation within plausible parameters of Quantum physics, relativity, and many other acceptable scientific theories, will exercise and stretch our minds, as we shall soon realize.

String Theory, Dark Matter, Dark Energy

Einstein got modern foundational physics going by developing his theories of relativity. His Nobel prizewinning theory on the photoelectric effect helped to move quantum physics forward, which is now responsible for approximately 1/3 of all modern-day technology. Quantum physics which he helped to kick start, works perfectly when describing sub-atomic aspects of reality. Einstein's relativity, works very well when describing visible, large scale phenomenon. Relativity and quantum physics however do not seem to play well with each other on their own specific size scales. Relativity keeps it big, while Quantum mechanics keeps it small. Physicists worldwide have worked to create a unified field theory in an effort to describe all phenomena from large to sub-atomically small, so far without much success.

Another scientific theory called sting theory claims to be able to provide a unified field theory to explain everything. String theory on the other hand proposes that all sub-atomic particles are made up of infinitesimally small charged energy strings that exist in at least eleven spacial dimensions. This theory was conceived decades ago, after extensive mathematical postulation of its plausibility, by means of imagination, insight, and logical creativity.

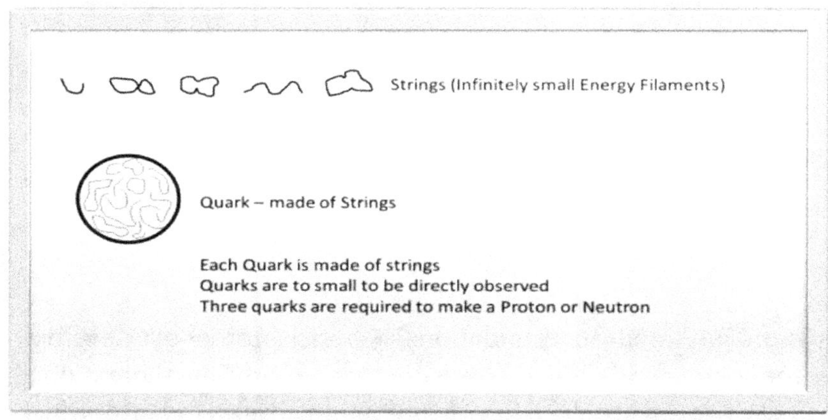

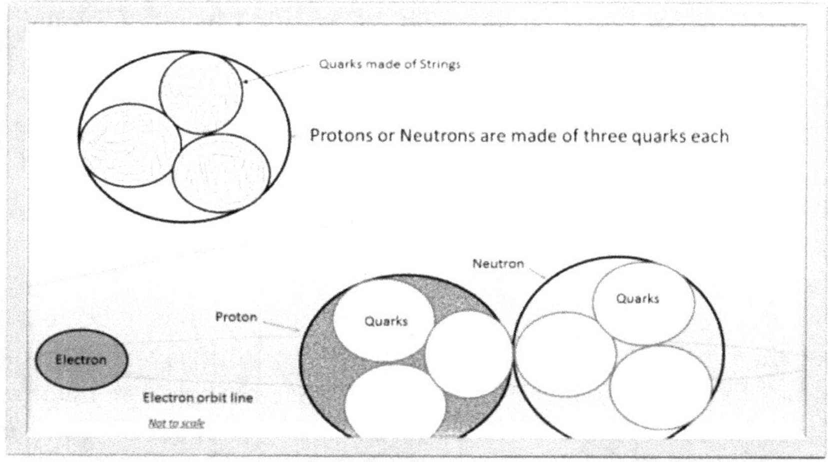

Einstein's relativity agreed that length, width, and depth dimensions create space in our three-dimensional world. He then added time as the fourth dimension, as a result of his work in developing the relativity papers. Relativity proclaims that we exist in a four-dimensional reality, which creates gravitational force by means of spacial distortion, caused by the density of massive matter based objects, which actually bends three-dimensional space down like a bowling ball on a trampoline mat, drawing other objects closer into the denser matter around its space. Relativity has been a solid player in physics, as it is now perceived as foundational law. Relativity has withstood the tests of time, and remains mathematically, and experimentally correct.

In order to visualize reality in a way that brings string theories eleven plus spacial dimensions into view, think of one of those illusionary focus puzzles you look at called magic eye artwork, with the dots and squiggles on a page that suddenly appear as an identifiable object, once one's visual focus falls out of attention. Only then can we see what the magic eye artist wanted us to see.

In order to see the Sting theory reality as it is meant to be seen, our focus must fall out from the normal status quo expectations, to allow a change of your perspective. The magic eye picture just looks like squiggles on the page, until your focus is in tune with the artistically engineered picture, that's why it's called the magic eye.

Reality is a lot like a magic eye picture in that our focus must be exactly as intended, for the real picture to show itself. A new way of thinking may be required for many of us, as well as an open mind, to attain required visual perspective, to understand string theory reality as an observational experience.

To understand that reality is constructed from more than eleven spacial dimensions, we may need to look at things we already understand differently. Looking beyond Einstein's four spacial dimensions relativity world will require a new perspective, and some convincing by means of understanding, and good thought experiments. Once the new perspective is established, and the mind opened to the logic of the discussion, the magic eye of reality will become clearer, and the string theory multi-dimensional reality will jump off of the page, and surprise you, just like the first magic eye picture you were able to understand as it was designed to be seen, by the observational experience it invokes.

An initial startup analogy for this discussion might be to think about your automobile, and how it gets you to work every day. Let's imagine an automobile represents our physical reality (far stretch but follow along please), and the automobile functions as required. Most individuals never question the automobiles working systems, as separate components of the whole vehicles reality. Most individuals just see the automobile, and know by turning the key, and pushing the gas pedal, it goes, where ever pointed to go. Multiple subsystems must work with each other in reality to result in a functional automobile, so it may perform as expected. Just ask your mechanic.

The drivetrain would not be enough to transport you anywhere, without the wheels, tires, and seats. The wheels would not do much good without the frame, drivetrain, and steering wheel. Without the seats, wiring harnesses, and controls, all of the technology would be useless. The entire automobile, together with all of its symbiotic parts make the whole, functional automobile, so that the car can work as expected.

The individual sub-systems which comprise the automobile are unaware of their contribution in the entire working machines functioning, they just do what they are designed to do without question. The automobile, just like our universal physical reality functions by means of cooperation, and entanglement the different (sub-assemblies) to make it function as required. Reality requires cooperation of (sub-assemblies) multiple spacial dimensions to function.

If we now imagine our physical reality broken down like the imaginary automobiles different sub-systems, and we open our minds to a new perspective, we may see that the many spacial dimensions of string theory present themselves to us, without any discrepancy to quantum mechanics, or Einstein's relativity theories. It may even seem elementary, after the new perspective is achieved by many of the readers at, or before the conclusion of this discussion.

With a new perspective on String Theory, it's easy to see that physical reality is indeed constructed by means of more than eleven spacial dimensions. These spacial dimensions work together while being entangled with each other to create our reality, just as the automobile systems work together (entangle) to make the vehicle function and become useful. The first step in convincing readers that we live in a multi-dimensional reality, is to define what a spacial dimension is. According to the Dictionary definition; of course. Not quite yet though, we need address something else first.

Step one; in our new way to perspective thinking exercise, is to forget that space is a three-dimensional aspect of reality. We need to imagine space as a single dimension, within itself. That's right think of space as just one dimension, for now. The dimension of Space which allows movement within itself, length, depth, and width are merely spacial dimensional parameters, of space, not extra dimensions in themselves. For string theory to work in this discussion, space will be a single spacial dimensional, nothing more, and nothing less; length, depth, and width create the single dimension of space.

Step two; is to imagine that time is just one dimension, consisting of past present, and future, which create the spacial aspect of time. No change there but I wanted to provide the new perspective on time and space, while both have specific parameters, but only represent two spacial dimensions together instead of four. This idea still agrees with Einstein, and relativity if one attempts to understand the bigger picture. (Agreeing with Einstein has been proven to be a smart thing to do throughout history) The time dimension is entangled with the space, dimension. Then before moving into the other spacial dimensions, we need to define what a spacial dimension actually is, in order to fill the requirements of a dimension, and proceed with our discussion on string theory's multi-dimensional reality.

String theory intends to explain the workings of our reality without the need for any mathematical constants, or band aids, like relativity requires in its limited parameters. Relativity never attempts to explain everything. But string theory should be able to bring quantum physics and the relativity theories into a unified field theory set of equations which consists of at least an 11 spacial dimensional created reality. This continues to elude status quo, mainline scientific thinking, and logic. Time passes, while reality changes understanding of itself.

String theory advocates, often state that the seven additional, elusive (hidden) dimensions, to our current four (space-time), are shrunk down so small, that they remain hidden from human detection. That said, humanity has been searching for these microscopic hidden dimensions, using any related scientific equipment that human technology can produce. The space and time dimensions we have already identified (agreed upon in science) do not seem to be limited in any way by size, length, depth, width, space, and time have no size restrictions, yet are spacial dimensions, and work with all required mathematical equations. Time and space also fall under the dictionary's definition of a (spacial) dimension.

We will now eliminate size as a spacial dimensional parameter (requirement), because reality is not small, time is not small, and space is not small. Since the spacial dimension is not small, we can deduce that any specific spacial dimension will not be hiding in a far-off corner of the universe, and still make a functional spacial dimension for string theory's functionality in describing reality. All of the spacial dimensions of string theory should be entangled with each other, similarly that time and space are entangled together. They should all be able to be used within mathematical equations of meaningful purpose, with proper symbolistic representations, just as space and time can be.

With all of that said, it's time to look at the requirements of a spacial dimension in our string theory discussion. We need to designate at least eleven spacial dimensions in order to initiate a meaningful string theory discussion. We will rely on the dictionary definition, of a dimension to proceed in our quest to dissect reality into its functional components.

Extra Dimensions

It's time to determine what it takes to be considered for a dimension. Several dictionaries were referenced, and combined, to provide a better overall definition of the word; dimensions.

<u>According to the dictionary.</u>

The definition of; dimension, reads as follows;
Dimensions are quantifiable.
Dimensions have a group of properties.
Dimensions have a level of existence.
Dimensions are fundamental units of reality.
Dimensions have a scope of magnitude.
Dimensions have a fundamental measure of physical quantity.
Dimensions are any number of independent parameters required to specify a quantifiable aspect of reality.

Dimensions, as defined in the dictionary, allow Time and Space fill all of the dictionary requirements to be considered dimensions in the String Theory discussion. Time has past, present, and future. Space has length, width, and depth. Both are fundamental aspect of reality.

Einstein opened humanities eyes with his relativity papers, and with a new perspective on (time) as the forth spacial dimension. It took 99% of the world's population an additional 14 years to understand, and accept what Einstein was talking about in his relativity papers with respect to his perspective on time.

When there was a solar eclipse that was carefully observed for light bending around the sun, fourteen years after his initial relativity publication. Teams of astronomers were able to prove that Einstein's theory of relativity was actually correct, and that gravity was able to bend light, and that time was in fact an actual dimension. It was now proven that mass induced gravity was able to bend space and light simultaneously. Up until that point in time, many people just thought that Einstein was an eccentric, or a bit crazy. Einstein then became world famous, almost overnight.

Afterwards a definitive explanation of gravity in a unified field theory of everything became Einstein's road block from that point forward. He spent the rest of his life attempting to complete his work on unifying gravity without success. He wanted gravity to fit into his pre-conceived notions of mathematical cooperation, within the framework of the other electromagnetic forces in nature. What we want in science is not what we always get, in reality. Einstein was a true scientist, he never gave up working on what he believed in.

Modern day string theory demands that there must be at least eleven spacial dimensions to work as a viable scientific unified field theory. This theory would have the ability to explain how reality functions, without any mathematical constants. We have already defined what is required to qualify as a spacial dimension, such as space, and time. Basically, dimensions are fundamental units a reality.

Let's make up a list of the spacial dimensions, and document the reasons that each one of the (dimensional) contestants should be considered as a spacial dimension. We will do this according to the dictionary definition of a dimension, and the plausible way that each fit into the engineering scheme of string theory's reality.

The formatting we will be using for this discussion, is to first define the dimensions as the dictionary does. We need to make sure the newly named dimensions, are actual dimensions according to the dictionary definitions of dimensions, before we can proceed. Then I will relate the dictionary definition of a dimension, to the newly named spacial dimension.

Then we will discuss how the newly defined dimension fits into our discussion of string theory. Remember that we are going into this discussion with our minds open, so that new ways of thinking are easier to accommodate. When theorizing at these levels, aspect of reality are neither provable, nor non-provable, and must be left to deduction, and logical reason within the parameters of what is known to be factual, and theoretically plausible. With that said. Let's go on a mind-bending journey together, into string theory's reality.

We will start with the familiar space and time spacial dimensions, making it easier to find perspective points on our journey, into open-minded discovery at the edge of reality.

1. Space – Cosmological spacial dimension

Space; is the infinite extension of length, width, and depth. Dimensional parameters that our reality is contained within, physically. Space has been defined as a three-dimensional place within which all matter in our universe resides.

In this exercise we will assign space as only a single spacial dimension, which will make more logical sense after the other dimensions are identified. It is thought that everything that exists, does so in space. In our new way of thinking about space and our reality, we will consider space to be a single dimension by logical definition.

This will also make it easier to envision the string theory model of dozens of spacial dimensions entangled, as the building blocks which create our reality. Space is the container in which all that we touch and see is confined. The container which holds the planets, stars, galaxies, even you and me.

Keep in mind that really open minded, new ways of thinking usually require adjustment time, and effort to settle in. Remember that Einstein's relativity theory took over a decade to be realized and accepted by the general public, and scientific communities. Then relativity gained traction due to a solar eclipse observation, making Einstein world famous overnight, after fourteen years in anticipation of his work. Einstein theorized that gravity could bend light, and space, and that mass created space curvature in which the gravity effect is created. His further definition of gravity with respect to unifying a field theory were halted, by relativity factors.

Space fits the existing criteria of a spacial dimension with ease. By dictionary definition space is quantifiable, and has a group of properties, length, width, and depth. Space has a level of existence, and is a fundamental aspect of reality. Remember that we are assigning space as only a single dimension in an effort to create a string theory working model with at least eleven spacial dimensions, which will allow string theory mathematicians to complete the proof verification work, without the need for mathematical constants to be used as band aids.

2. Sub-Space – Cosmological spacial dimension

Our spacial dimension contains hidden parameters, or extensions into the inverted mirror image of space itself, this is to be called sub-space. Think of an inverted space that exists, just like our consciousness has a sub-consciousness underneath, that we cannot directly make contact with. Just as we are aware of matter and anti-matter, science will soon discover the sub-space dimension which is just out of sight of present day detection equipment.

The sub-spacial dimension (a universe) is where the missing universal anti-matter resides. Matter resides in the spacial dimension (our universe). Anti-matter resides in the sub-spacial dimension. The sub-space dimension is as much a part of reality, as our space dimension is, once the larger picture is factored in; String Theory reality, this will make logical sense to most readers. Keep an open mind as we dive in.

To visualize the sub-spacial dimension, imagine drawing a 3D black outline of a cube on a blank page of paper, which has a corner to corner distance of three inches. Then imagine tracing lines from all eight corners of the 3D cube into the cubes CenterPoint. Then imagine with orange ink, extending the eight lines from the center point the same distance beyond center point, then completing the orange cube (into sub-space), in the same space as the original cube. The sub-spacial dimension is the inversion of the spacial dimension in which we reside.

In this thought experiment one is able to imagine the manner in which the sub-space dimension exists in the same place as spacial dimension without interference with each other. Sub-Space is an inverted spacial dimension filled with anti-matter, creating a universal domain that mirrors our spacial reality. For every atom of matter in the universe, there exists an anti-matter atom to balance it for required mathematical stability. They cannot make direct contact without annihilation, so reality creates an invisible (to our senses) veil between dimensions.

The sub-spacial dimension entangles directly with conscious imagination. Space and Sub-Space give purpose to reality as they entangle with the multi-dimensional aspect of living conscious observation. Sub-space balances space in the energy give and take of universal reality (more on this later). Hang in there, we are just getting started. Keep the mind open, take in the entire discussion, it gets complex, exciting, thought provoking, yet remains balanced.

Sub-Space and space are not permitted to exist in the same dimensional contact simultaneously, without severe penalties of annihilation payments due. Think about what happens to matter and anti-matter when they come into direct contact with each other, its annihilation.

The universal perimeter bow shock Nexus wave front, and the center of black hole singularities attest to the consequence of spacial and sub-spacial dimensional meetings, face to face. [Primer; more on Nexus, and singularities phenomenon later in this discussion.]

3. Time - Cosmological spacial dimension

Time is the measure of change which allows humanity to catalog its history. Time is a measurement parameter which is useful in determining trajectories, destinations, project deadlines, and birthday parties, as well as many other aspects of daily life.

On this planet time is based on a twenty-four-hour planetary rotation cycle for convenience sake. We sub-divide the earth day into 24 definable temporal units called hours, with additional sub-divisions of minutes and seconds to allow accurate, within reason tracking and scheduling for consumerism, and spiritual conveniences. Science utilizes additional sub-divisions of seconds for precise experimentation and prediction science, called Plank Time.

Humans are able to adapt Applied Physics to these temporal divisions for mathematical calculations which are relevant to time concerns with respect to engineering technologies, and full moon, and solar eclipse phases, airplane arrivals, picking up the kids after school, anniversaries, etc.

Time keeping on a different planet might require mathematical adaptations to create logical calculations with respect to maintaining accurate engineering solutions, rotational cycles and gravity strength. Equations can be designed to accommodate any temporal scenario imaginable, with logic. Time is relative, and subject to observational situations in many ways, according to Einstein's relativity works.

When looking through any telescope at a star in the sky, the observer is observing the star in the past, relative to the distance the star is from the observation. A star that is ten light years away is observed as it was ten years ago, at the time of the observation. What the observer is watching, is not what is actually happening at the time of observation, from the perspective of the observed object.

Absolute time across any considerable distance becomes impossible from the observation point, due to reality's relativity parameters. The stars light takes ten years to travel to the observer in the thought experiment, so the observer sees the light that left the star ten years ago. The star may have died since the light left it ten years ago, but the observer would not be able to verify that for up to another ten years, due to the distance of observation, and finite speed that light travels that distance through the spacial dimension.

Light travels about four trillion miles in a year, which is the universal speed limit for almost anything that travels through space. The universe (does) allow faster than light speed travel, for a traveler who is not traveling through the (spacial dimension). This will become significant in later discussion of the outer edges of the actual universe.

Time travel is a science fiction dream come true for many movie producers, and goers. Time travel is not impossible according to relativity mathematical equations. Unfortunately, time travel is beyond current technology levels, and seems to be years away from our reality.

Before humanity embarks on a time travel mission we should take care to remember the grandfather paradox that Einstein warned us about. It states that if you traveled back in time, and met your grandfather, and then somehow prevented him from meeting your grandmother, you would never have been born in the first place, so we better be careful in such an endeavor as actual time travel.

Convincing all of you that time is a viable spacial dimension is easy, due to the fact that Einstein has already done it, and so far, he has been correct in all of his physics theories.

But in keeping to the format we're using; the dictionary definition of time must be utilized for each spacial dimension in our string theory discussion.

Time is quantifiable, and it has a group of properties, and is a fundamental aspect of reality, and has a level of existence. Remember it took fourteen years for the humans on this planet to agree with Einstein's relativity papers on time. We are modern humans and more open minded to new ideas and logic, than most were a hundred years ago, right?

Einstein's thought experiments were legendary, saved time and money, and utilized pure logical deduction to find solutions, within the imagination. Time entangles dimensionally with all spacial dimensions as the fundamental measuring stick of evolutionary status. Times enigmatic parameters with respect to gravity, velocity, and relativity allows, reality to exist in a natural state consistent with universal spacial dimensions which are beyond average human comprehension at this stage in evolution.

Time and space create universal divisions of spacial dimensional barriers, which prevent ignorant intelligent species from interacting with each other in a protective manner, thereby preventing confrontational matters of war and conquest, before said species evolves sufficiently to avoid such catastrophe's, as a result of ignorant technological advances.

Now we have covered the already recognized two spacial dimension of space and time, with sub-space added as the third spacial dimension. Some may consider the sub-space addition non-relevant at this time, but just give it a little more time. It will become recognizable later in this discussion, as reality becomes defined in its complexities, with respect to the multi-dimensional string theory applications of this discussion.

Time to add some new spacial dimensions to our discussion.

4. Gravity - cosmological spacial dimension

Gravity; is the attractive force between any sufficiently large matter based objects, which acts on all other matter within its field of influence. Gravitational force is proportional to the square of the distance between the relative objects, with respect to their masses. Gravity is an electromagnetic force which is developed by means of massive amounts of matter which entangle within space surrounding thereby creating a curved dimple in the space and time dimensions, which in turn allows surrounding matter to fall towards the larger mass object. Gravity allows matter to clump and eventually grow in size to become planets and stars. Gravity pulls on all matter, light, and space.

Gravity on the earth dictates very specific applied physics mathematical formulas that are different on other planets, which have different gravitational attractions. Gravity controls solar system, and galactic movements, and has done so for all of time that the universe has existed. Space-time gravitational attraction seems to have been designed with respect to its perfection, in the amount of force it relatively possesses.

If gravity was any amount stronger, the universe would have clumped into very large stars with no planetary development. If gravity was any weaker than it is, the stars and planets would not have developed, and you would not be reading this theoretical paper, or any other paper for that matter, because you and I would not exist.

Einstein spent a large part of his life-time attempting to make gravity fit into his electromagnetic mathematical equations, and fit a preconceived model of his elusive grand unified field theory of everything, without satisfaction. With an open mind, and our new way of thinking about reality, we can see that gravity fits into the category of a spacial dimension, for a string theory discussion into the edge of reality.

Einstein added time to our dimensional list with his relativity equations, but was unable to fit gravity into the mix, in all the excitement. Remember that he was also working to understand the quantum physics field that he may have inadvertently discovered, or reinforced along the way. While his thought experimental partner Neils Bohr was able to comprehend the quantum mechanical field, Einstein remained perplexed by its illogical stance. Quantum enigmas may have hindered Einstein's ability to focus on the gravitational relationships, within the equations he encountered.

Defining gravity within the parameters of a dictionary dimensional definition is next.

Gravity; is quantifiable. Gravity is a fundamental aspect of reality, and has a level of existence. Gravity has a fundamental measure of physical quantity. Gravity has a scope of magnitude. Gravity has a fundamental measure of physical quantity; as much as space and time do. Gravity thereby fits all dictionary definitional requirement to be called a spacial dimension, for our open-minded String Theory discovery discussion.

Gravity entangles with the other spacial dimensions in a direct manner with respect to space and time, and other dimensions that we will be discovering in this discussion. Gravity creates stars, galaxies and even the mysterious black hole singularities, that science fiction like to portray as dangerous machines for time travel, and wormholes.

A sneak peek into the future of this discussion will show that gravitational forces in the center of singularities, is strong enough to crush disassembled neutron compacted matter into anti-matter, while squeezing it into the sub-spacial dimension instantaneously.

The initial gravity created by the big bang explosion bow shock (Nexus Wave) wave front entangles (super-gravity) throughout the physical universe like a spherical magnet, which is continuously expanding at twice the speed of light, which draws all matter in an outward manner. (More on this will be discussed in detail with the Nexus Wave, Supergravity and Singularity sections of this discussion.)

Gravity exists in fractal increments in our reality which is involved in dozens of spacial dimensions, both seen and unseen. As string theory scientists continue to seek the required minimum of eleven spacial dimensions. They often say that the additional dimensions are very small and curled up in our reality out of sight.

I like to think about that when pondering the size of length, or depth, of width, or even the size of time. The spacial dimensions I am pondering in this thought experiment do not have size parameter restrictions, and should not have size parameters restrictions, and do not need size parameters restrictions to qualify as spacial dimensions, according to the dictionary definition of a dimension.

The final sales pitch for allowing gravity to fit into the spacial dimensional category, is that gravity is used in countless mathematical calculation formulas. Without gravitational mathematic equations, much of our modern day applied physics technology could not function.

The open-minded scientist can agree that in our new way of thinking gravity is a spacial dimension, which is required to verify the String Theory discussion resolution.

5. *Light (electromagnetic radiation) Cosmological spacial Dimension*

Electromagnetic radiation from stars permeates the entire physical universe. This radiation gives life to our reality, and allows humans to exist. The visible light which humans can detect, or see, allows human senses to observe reality. Light exists due to the entanglement of space, time, gravity, and matter, which have worked together to create stars in the universe.

Electromagnetic radiation (which I will just call *light* from here on in, to simplify the discussion) is composed of varying frequencies of electromagnetic energy which in turn determine lights energy content levels. Stars emit light in a very wide bandwidth of frequencies simultaneously, from high energy to low intensity. Stars radiate light in the form of cosmic radiation, which is the highest group of energy carrying frequencies, and most destructive. Gamma and X-ray radiation are also radiated by all stars and carry sufficient energy to destroy life as we know it, due to their high energy contents. Then we have the frequency range of ultra-violet, infrared, and visible light which are beneficial to humans and animals, and allow natural eye sight for many species on earth. Next on the light frequency list are radio waves and micro waves which benefit human technology more than the others kinds of light.

Light energy from the sun initiates life on our planet through means of photosynthesis in plants. Earth plants then become food for the animals and insects which inhabit earth along with humans, you and me. Light from stars feeds life on the surrounding planets, if the environment allows it to do so. Light is life's energy source for the most part. It is safe to say that light gives life to the earth.

Light fits into our new way of thinking model very well to be considered a spacial dimension, for the open-minded scientist who is searching for the dimensional String Theory parameters. Light, like time exists in our physical reality which takes care of the spacial aspect of the defined spacial dimension.

Light; is quantifiable, has a group of properties, has a level of existence, and is a fundamental unit of reality. Light has a scope of magnitude, and a fundamental measure of physical quantity. Light has any number of independent parameters required to specify a quantifiable aspect of reality. Light fills all requirements as a spacial dimension in the dictionary definition of a dimension, for the open minded and new thinking scientific theorists.

Light moves through space faster than any material thing can, man-made or natural. The speed of light is used in mathematical calculations, and is imperative to the laws of physics as we understand them. Light speed and energy, which light is, are required for the relativity equations. $E=MC^2$, Light thereby meets all justifiable requirement to be considered a spacial dimension for our string Theory discussion. Without lights energy and speed parameters, Einstein's relativity papers could not exist.

Light travels more than six trillion miles in one year, which is referred to as one light year. Traveling any faster than light, and one breaks the time continuity barrier, thereby moving backwards in time by means of super velocity. Relativity mathematics, though dictates that traveling faster than light is not permitted physically. Light photons have no mass, yet contain energy through shear velocity according to relativity equations.

As any matter based object approaches light speed, its mass increases at an exponential rate, while its length decreases in a directional manner simultaneously; thereby forbidding any object to obtain light speed, as a matter of fact.

In other words, as one approaches light speed one shrinks in length as it become infinitely heavy. At light speed one would be flat and as heavy as the universe, thereby preventing it (light speed) from physically occurring. In a manner of speaking, time seems to be a partner to light, space and matter.

Light is not merely limited to the physical universe as we understand it, but also exists in our imagination, and sub-conscious dreams. Light entangles with conscious living nervous systems to provide eye sight, warmth on the skin, and even a sun tan. Humans even derive certain life-giving vitamins (D vitamins) through sun light absorption.

Light entangles with consciousness which allows sight. Light reflects into an array of situations which change perspective for observation.

Imagine looking at the water in a pond. Notice the water and the waves that the breeze creates on the water's surface. By adjusting your visual focus you may now notice that the water's surface is also reflecting the clouds, trees and flowers in the background, from behind the pond, for your sight to enjoy the observation.

Then you notice the colorful fish swimming just below the surface of the pond waters. This new perspective may have eliminated the surface reflections you were just enjoying simultaneously.

Next a little boy standing by the pond throws a rock into the water causing waves that distort all of the things that you were just observing in the water, and reflecting on the surface of it simultaneously. Light and conscious perspective have varying degrees of observational relativity.

With the assistance of light, you were able to observe three different visual aspects of the same situation (the pond), or three layers, or three-dimensional perspectives of the same situation. Light is responsible for the reflective, and penetrational aspects of matter, which allow the perspective observational choices when looking at water for the human eyes to see, and the human consciousness to think about. Just as X-ray light allows sight into solid matter (x-ray of broken arm), the conscious imagination allows sight into the sub-spacial dimension, due to light.

Light carries spectrographically decipherable information after reflecting off distant planet atmospheres, which can be interpreted by means of spectral frequency analysis technology. Humans can determine the distant planets atmospheric elements with this technology of light.

If human sight allowed full light spectrum vision, our reality would be a frightening place to observe as we would see through solid objects and be unable to decipher one thing from another. Humans would look like spirit creatures to each other, as we would see through our own bodies' electromagnetic fields, as angelic creatures. One might think that they were in the sub-space, anti-matter dimension if our sight were that good.

Light fits the criteria for our string theory quest, as a spacial dimension without question. We now are looking at five spacial dimensions, even though we took space from three dimensions down to one dimension, so let's keep things moving forward. One step backwards, allows three steps forward.

6. Matter -Cosmological spacial Dimension

Matter is composed of any of over one hundred basic elementary compounds which we call elements. Elements are made up of molecules, which are a combination of different atoms. Atoms are a combination of protons, neutrons, and electrons in specific ratios. Each proton and neutron is made up of three sub-atomic particles called quarks. Other sub-atomic particles exist in large numbers, which combine to make up atomic matter. String theory suggests that sub-atomic particles are constructed from tiny strings of pure energy (light).

Matter makes up everything that we can touch, and most of what we can see. Matter is the foundation of reality, which without we would not be. We live within a matter based reality.

Matter is the solid building block of our reality. Stars, planets, and people are made of matter. Matter is the foundation of reality. Quantum mechanics seems to enjoy the enigmatic. Viewing matter in the quantum mechanical aspect, matter is made up of very little solid matter, if any at all.

On the sub-atomic scale (atoms) consist of protons and neutron at their nucleus which are very small in comparison to the entire atoms size. The electrons which circle the atom in specific spherical shells, are a hundred thousand times farther away from the atomic nucleus, than the diameter of the nucleus itself. The electron is a thousand time smaller than the protons and neutrons alike.

To get an understanding of the amount of space to matter ratio within a single atom, let's do a thought experiment. Imagine that all of the atoms in your body were suddenly compressed to a point that left no space between the protons, neutrons (Atomic Nucleus) and electrons (Orbiting the Atomic Nucleus) in every atom in your body. All of the compressed atoms in your body would then fit onto the area of the period, at the end of this sentence.

Hard to believe, isn't it? That's one of the reasons that physics have been looking so hard, to find the Higgs boson (God Particle) that which is believed to give mass to all matter. Scientist think that the very tiny Higgs Boson could be everywhere like a soup, which provides resistance normal sized sub-atomic particles as they move in space. The Higgs particles then could explain how mass is obtained by sub-atomic matter.

Other scientist think that the Holographic Principle might hold the mysterious answer to the question how does matter obtain mass. The Holographic Principle states that (reality) is nothing more than a digital holographic projection of some sort. This group of scientists has a genius amongst them who was able to do a mathematical proof to that conclusion, wow! Many scientists dismiss the holographic principle as non-sense.

For the open-minded thinker, matter fits our definition of a spacial dimension with great precision. Matter; is quantifiable, it has a group of properties, and a level of existence, and is a fundamental unit of reality. Matter has a scope of magnitude, and a measure of physical quantity. Matter meets all criteria to be considered as a spacial dimension for this string theory discussion, for the open minded scientifically curious readers, at the edge of reality.

Matter entangles directly with space, time, gravity, and light. Matter entangles with anti-matter in particle acceleration experiments, and super nova evens in our spacial dimensional universe. Equal amounts of anti-matter exist in the sub-space dimension, as matter in the spacial dimension. Just as space, and sub-space are opposite aspects of dimensional reality. Matter and anti- matter are opposite aspects of dimensional reality in that they cannot occupy the same dimensional space simultaneously. Matter and anti-matter are balanced in reality, as a matter of mathematical existence, without flexibility- (scientific law). They are not permitted to exist simultaneously in the same spacial dimension, without destructive consequences, of annihilation.

Anti-Matter – is composed of anti-particles, especially antiprotons, antineutrons, and positrons. Anti-matter particles have the same mass, and spin as matter counter particles, but have opposite values with respect to all other quantum nonzero numbers. When anti-matter particles contact matter particle, total annihilation results and only energy remains as a result. Anti-matter is in quantity balance universally, as matter occupies spacial dimensions, and anti-matter occupies sub-spacial dimensions, almost exclusively.

According to sting theory these foundational sub-atomic particles, matter or anti-matter, are composed of combinations of tiny energy string filaments, which can be open ended strings, or closed loops string of various configuration, which combine in specific ratios to create sub atomic particles, like quarks. In other words, all matter is constructed of energy strings and nothing more.

7. Mathematics -Cosmological spacial Dimension

Mathematics; is logic, the absolute search and statements, using numbers and symbols. The field of study of numbers, arrangements, and relationship using (rigorously defined) (operational symbols). Mathematics is consisting of arithmetic, geometry, algebra, trigonometry, calculus, thermodynamics, electronics, chemistry, physics, etc., while new discoveries occur with time. Mathematics is the foundation of all technology. It is the foundation from which humanity forged out of the Stone Age. All of mathematics exists presently and always has, but is yet to be fully realized by human consciousness.

Mathematics fits into the category of a spacial dimension, in that it exists within the universe. Mathematics has a level of existence, and a group of properties. Mathematics is a fundamental unit of reality. It has a scope of magnitude, and a fundamental measure of physical quantity. Mathematics is used to verify dimensional existence as a means of proof. Mathematics is a spacial dimension by definition, to the open-minded individual who embraces a new way of thinking in order to discover a deeper sense of reality in the heart of string theory, which entangles quantum physics with relativity to unify our universal conscious understanding of reality.

Mathematics has a direct entanglement with all cosmological spacial dimensions, as well as creating technology. Mathematics has an indirect entanglement with life's consciousness, communication, imagination, observational relativity. Mathematics can be seen as the tree of knowledge, if one imagines that Mathematics as the tree trunk with a number of primary branches such as geometry, algebra, geometry, calculus, fluid dynamics, etc., which have secondary branches growing off of each primary branch as specialty, and specific mathematical equations.

Mathematical tree of knowledge grows with conscious understanding of universal mathematical principles. In actual reality the mathematical tree of knowledge is a fractal giant to which a man is able to discover a branch at a time. Information collected by nature's black hole event horizon (information paradox) is likely in the mathematical format, maybe not just in human mathematical language of base-ten numbers and defined symbols; remember the movie contact.

The method of other species specific mathematical language communication may vary from human understanding. Mysterious crop circles come to my mind, as many of them give resemblance to higher fractal mathematical equations, and even the Mandelbrot sets series, are evident in some of the crop circle designs, seen over the years around our planet earth.

The real question might be, are humans as intelligent as they think they are? The world is after all, always at war with each other in some place or another, for questionable reasons.

All spacial dimensions of string theory containing mathematical proof of existence, and function whether realized at this time, or yet to be realized at some time in the future, are sound. Once accepted it is just a matter of time, until the proofs are completed by earth's higher mathematicians. Humanities brightest mathematicians always define logic with their accomplishments, while the rest of us watch in amazement.

Mathematics is the universal language. Regardless of formatting, symbols, or text language, and will likely be the common languages between alien races, once a common symbolic structure is established, such as our base-ten numbers then we could agree upon the universal symbol set to match, ex. E=energy, M=mass, C=light speed, E=MC^2.

Mathematics; is the explanation of relationships which occur in reality, with respect to observation and observer, the basic communications and shared symbolic list of intelligent language formatting.

Mathematics concerning aspects of reality such as consciousness, or imagination fall short with direct relation to numeric interpretation and fitting equations, due to their sentient nature. Just as aptitude exams, or employment aptitude test require translation templates, for which probability statistics are applied, to determine compatibility parameters.

So are the mathematical equations hidden which will be derived for the sentient spacial dimensions of string theory. These new equations will be more complex than relativity's E=MC^2. New areas of mathematics await discovery, as humanity's best minds work out the new thinking models to accommodate string theories multidimensional reality which we inhabit. Just as humanity thrives with hundreds of languages worldwide, it will continue to discover new mathematical formats with the evolution of time.

A historic genius such a Ramanujan may have already left the mathematic equations in his personal note books, we'll see. Mathematics brings our spacial dimension count up to seven, let's keep it going.

8. *Motion -Cosmological spacial Dimension*

Motion; is the change of position of anything relative to anything else. All matter in reality, is in motion relative to itself and something else. Distance change between objects creates motion. All subatomic matter is in a constant state of high speed motion.

Does motion fit into the category of a spacial dimension? Motion occurs in the physical universe. Motion is quantifiable, it contains a group of properties, span, velocity, direction, consistency. Motion is a fundamental unit of reality, everything is in motion. Motion has a scope of magnitude. Motion has a fundamental measure of physical quantity, velocity. Motion has a level of existence, as much as time does. Motion does meet the criteria to be labeled a spacial dimension in our quest for string theory resolution.

All spacial dimensions are entangled with motion, time flows, space expands, force causes motion, light travels, gravity pulls, matter moves, mathematics developing equations. Reality is in a constant cosmological and subatomic dance, the entire physical universe is in motion with the predictable precision of a Swiss watch, and has been in this logical motion since the big bang.

Planetary motions in temporal rotation standardize time units are incurred. Motion dictates change, which is the foundation of times entanglement from tiny subatomic super strings, to massively large superstructure galactic webs. Motion is applicable to every aspect of reality. Everything changes, nothing stays the same.

Even the stationary object on that table in front of you is in motion, as its atoms move inside the table, and the table moves through space with the earth's rotation, and the earth's movement around the sun, as the sun moves around the galaxy, and the galaxy moves through the universe.

As you are sitting in your chair reading this discussion the earth is spinning at about a thousand miles an hour, at the equator. Your position on the earth relative to the equator will change your speed as you move with the planet from a thousand to almost zero if you were at the polar rotational axis points.

As the planet produces movement for you spinning, it is also traveling around the sun at about 66,000 mph. The sun and solar system are also traveling through the Milky Way galaxy at about 45,000 mph. Which is added to the other numbers to give relative speed of your position.

However, the Milky Way galaxy is also moving through the universe, which is difficult to determine accurately due to the fact that everything else in the universe is moving also. Scientist have measured the other galaxies around the Milky Way, and determined that it might be moving as fast as 2,237,000 mph.

Using that estimated rate of motion, we can say that while just sitting in your chair reading this paper, you may be moving at around 2,855,000 mph. Scientist think that the universe might also be moving, which would increase the speed of motion that we are all currently doing.

To take it a step further let's think about the direction that we are moving in the bigger picture as we discuss interesting things here. The earth is spinning, (1000 mph) and within that spinning motion we are also circling the sun (67,000 mph), while the galaxy is rotating at (45,000), and rotating through the universe at (2,237,000 mph). That means that if viewed from afar we would be doing spirals within spirals, within spirals, as we move at around through space at about 2,855,000 mph, or roughly 800 miles per second, through the spacial dimension.

Just sitting there looking at the object on the table in front of you, finds you both moving at least a couple of million miles per hour, and doing so in several different sized spiral loops simultaneously. The atoms in matter move in vibrational motion, as their electrons circle at tremendous speed around each atomic nucleus. We see that everything is in motion, and moves relative to everything else.

9. *Force -Cosmological spacial Dimension*

Force; is the ability to change energy, to initiate change of motion. The action to overcome material inertia. Capacity to work, causing change, a vector quantity that produces an acceleration of any-body in the direction of its application. To move against resistance. To effect or impose ones will upon another.

Forced fits into the category of a spacial dimension. Force is quantifiable, has a group of properties, and has a level of existence. Forces is a fundamental unit of reality, it exists in the universe and within reality just like space, time, gravity, light, matter, and motion do. Force has a scope of magnitude, and a measure of physical quantity, thereby fulfilling all requirements to be labeled a spacial dimension in our quest to resolve string theory multi-dimensional requirements.

The measure of force is utilized in many different mathematical formulas to calculate solutions in many different fields of study, and engineering alike. Force is calculated in motor and engine designs.

Gravity is an electromagnetic force. Inertia is a stored-up force. Engines produce machine, or physical force.

Force was initiated by gravity when stars formed. Force was reborn as stars ignited, and more so when they die in a super nova explosion. Stellar accretion discs form planets and meteors which can cause collisions, creating unpredictable forces which can cause cascading situations.

Force entangles with the spacial dimensions of motion, gravity, mathematics, matter, etc., allowing reality to function as we understand it. Force interacts with nine other spacial dimensions indirectly. Force is a result of spacial dimension entanglements in our reality. Force can be manufactured and exploited in such technological devices has engines and machines. Force and gravity entangles within black hole singularity's causing the matter ingested to be entangled back into Anti-matter in the sub-space dimension, where it originally came from. It can be said that gravity is a force with accuracy, but momentum is also a force, as is light, and sound which are created in different ways than gravity is created. Force is a resultant action of effort, work, or chemistry.

10. Temperature- Cosmological spacial Dimension

Temperature; is the scalar quantity of heat or coldness in an object or defined space. Temperature is usually defined in degrees of Fahrenheit, Celsius or Kelvin depending on the mathematical application of observation. As a temperature in matter increases so does the vibrational frequency of the sub-atomic particles within the matter being observed.

Temperature fits into the category of a spacial dimension because it exists in all of matter in the universe. Temperature is quantifiable, and it contains a group of properties. Temperature has a level of existence, and is a fundamental unit of reality. Temperature has a scope of magnitude, and has a measure of physical quantity. Temperature meets all criteria to be categorized as a spacial dimension in our quest for string theory resolution. Temperature (scalar quantities) are required in many mathematical computations of physics and thermodynamics equations alike.

Keeping an open mind to the string theory discussion, we begin to see the magic eye picture of reality being unveiled before our eyes. By changing the visual focus, we can change perspective on a topic, which allows a new way of seeing it. Not everything is as it seems after a little bit of time walking around while observing it. Things can appear different from the back than they do from the front. Observing reality from the back, instead of the front (status quo) reveals a different side of the equation for individual observational perspectives.

Temperature entangles directly with matter, mathematics, force, motion, gravity, space, etc. Temperature entangles indirectly with everything in reality, even your mood.

Temperature fluctuations in the universal spacial dimension can range from -462° F, in deep space, to around 23 billion degrees within the core of large stars. Temperature mathematically dictates various forms of matter, gas, liquid, solid, plasma, etc.

Our reality was formed through chemistry and temperature by means of hydrogen fusion in stars which eventually created all elements up to plutonium, by means of gravity, time and chemistry. Entanglement through means of gravity, matter, temperature, space, time, mathematics, and chemistry.

Human body temperature is limited to within a few degrees of 98° F, for life to continue. Specific temperature range is applied, for all material performance parameters in reality. Water becomes a different material with different temperature applications, as do most elements. Temperature has the ability to transform matter based states as a function of reality.

11. Chemistry - Cosmological spacial Dimension

Chemistry; is the elements of a complex entity like a star and their relationship, the composition, structure, properties and reactions of a substance. Reactions of atoms and molecules which create new substances or materials.

The initial universe contained hydrogen and helium. Gravity coalesced these simple compounds eventually into stars which burn hydrogen and helium. At the end of the stars lifetime helium is converted by heat and pressure into lithium, and then into the Beryllium, and then to boron, into carbon, and oxygen then into sodium, magnesium, silicon, sulfur, argon, and then into the heavier elements that we are used to using for technology on earth.

All of the heavier than Helium elements on the earth, were formed in dyeing stars long ago by means of chemistry. All of the elements in the human body initially came from dyeing stars long ago, in other words you and I are made of prehistoric star dust matter. Chemistry is at the heart of reality, with without it, our material reality would not exist.

Chemistry fits into our criteria for a spacial dimension as it exists in the universe from cosmology, and geology, to life itself. Because of chemistry everything that is made of matter, is.

Chemistry has a group of properties, and it is a fundamental unit of reality. Chemistry has a scope of magnitude, and a fundamental measure of physical quantity. By definition chemistry is a spacial dimension in our quest to resolve string theory's explanation of reality.

Chemistry entangles directly with matter, pressure, time, space, temperature, and basically everything we know. Chemistry acts naturally as a chef in a kitchen (space), preparing a meal as it cooks up a cosmological reality, fit for conscious life with only hydrogen and helium as its initial ingredients. Gravity, space, and time being its culinary tools, provided to create within, chemistry cooks up reality.

Chemistry actually initiates within our spacial universe at the (Nexus wave front) as anti-matter particles are entangled, and transformed into matter particles as they move from the sub-spacial dimension, into our spacial dimension through the high velocity passing of the expanding Nexus wave front at our universal bow shock wave shells' perimeter.

Chemistry created humanity through the multi-dimensional evolution, now conscious life creates technology through the entanglement of chemistry and the multidimensional reality that we that reside within.

Chemistry from the metallurgy of the bronze age, into astrophysics spectrometry which detects through light entanglement the material elements of distant Xo-planets planet atmospheres, into medicine and advanced materials for commerce. Humans and their technology picked up where nature, and god left off.

Chemistry within life's cellular structure, and its symbiotic mitochondria, functioning's are beyond most human understanding, and yet are required for life to exist. Stomach gut bacteria works to aid in food digestion without knowledge of its functioning. DNA provides chemical instruction to matter based cells to become specific tools for bodily functioning without knowledge of individual operational parameters required to allow the whole body to function, chemistry. Chemistry entangles with matter providing functionality throughout reality.

Inside of every living human cell, are hundreds of chemical reactions occurring independent of the other body cells, yet acting correctly, entangled in quantum packets, directed chemically by nerve commands.

83 trillion individual human cells in your body are alive by means of over 100 chemical reactions in each cell commencing simultaneously. That means that approximately 8.3 quadrillion individual chemical reactions are occurring simultaneously inside the human body without considering the electro chemical nervous system being involved. This chemistry provides the living essence for life to host consciousness within itself.

In my final effort to convince any hold out individuals that chemistry is a spacial dimension, consider the following. Chemistry is an engineering aspect of reality, and utilizes mathematical calculations in its endeavor when working within its field which are a requirement. Without chemistry the universe would not be able to evolve into a life-giving reality.

Chemistry is the mathematical trading of sub-atomic particles and energy expenditures to enhance and change the nature of matter, in time and space.

Chemistry added to the spacial dimensions chart counts at eleven, just enough dimensions for the Brainiac mathematicians to complete the string theory equations. Eleven spacial dimensions is the minimum amount for string theory requirements. We're going for the maximum amount in this discussion. Remember, open minded thinking, New ways of seeing reality.

We're just getting started though, string theory allows dozens of dimensions to exist. It has mathematical provisions to allow them as well. They are expected in other words, so let's keep moving forward, and with our open minds in tacked. We're just getting warmed up, stay with me. The discussion keeps getting better as we impregnated deeper into realities wonders.

Thus far in our string theory discussion of additional spacial dimensions, we have been addressing the basic cosmological spacial dimensions of the matter based universe. The matter based universe existed long before any sentient life forms were around to observe and enjoy its creation. In the next section of our discussion we will be addressing the sentient spacial dimensions in which we exist, as an extension to the string theory requirements on the multi-dimensional reality we see, and in we be. By definition, dimensions are not limited by parameters of size or limited consistency.

12. Life- #1 Sentient spacial Dimension

Life; is the property which distinguishes organisms from matter. Life containing metabolism, growth, reproduction, and responsive to stimuli. Human and animal physical and spiritual experiences that constitute conscious awareness, are results of life. Life is the result of inception, and species diversification.

Human life is an entanglement of brain, nervous system, lymphatic system, circulatory system, respiratory system, digestive system, skeletorial system, skin, glands, which all combine with sensory systems, which entangle within the brains multiple symbiotic systems to achieve conscious awareness, by means of chemical electrical interactions throughout the entire multi-faceted body system.

Life is the time when something functions, or exists. A life is aware of its existence whether it be a plant or an animal or even a bacterial system.

To be a living human being is to experience reality through the body's many systems, while being able to question its own existence and ponder the meaning of life itself. Experiencing life with consciousness, which allows experiences to be enjoyed, and repeated for fun. Life is an elusive aspect of reality, as it is hard to define and distinguish when interrogated, but undeniable when experienced.

Life fits into the category of a spacial dimension by definition alone. Life is quantifiable, and has a group of properties. Life has a level of existence, and is a fundamental aspect of reality. Without the sentient spacial dimension of life, the universe would have little meaning. Life meets all dictionary definitional requirements. In our quest to initiate string theory as the unified field theory that explains reality and how it works, and in our new way of thinking.

Open minded objectivity is required, when dealing with complex and controversial topics. Remember how long it took for humanity to accept time as a new dimension (space-time), after Einstein created his relativity papers in 1904. It took over ten years.

Life is entangled directly with the spacial dimensions of, well all of them. Without life reality would have no purpose. Life is a sentient spacial dimension. Sentient dimensions entangle on a level of conscious awareness, whereas cosmological dimensions interact and entangle through natural reaction to each other.

An example would be chemistry, which requires matter, time, and space to occur. All spacial dimensions can entangle with all other spacial dimensions, situational observation specifically. Reality is complex and involved with uncountable reactions and entanglements in its activities.

Life creates opportunity to entangle with reality in a matter based spacial dimensionally ongoing dynamic situational experience. Life gives rise to free will to interactivness within an entangled matter-based reality. Just like space provides a place for the other cosmological spacial dimensions to reside, life does the same for its communal symbiotic sentient spacial dimensions as we will discover shortly.

Initially, a long time ago in history, life consciously entangled with matter based elements, and bacteria, initiating itself with the cosmological spacial dimension of matter. Mineral bacteria initially took root by entangling with light, matter, chemistry and time.

Bacteria then evolved into multi cellular organisms as a matter of mathematical efficiency, trial and error. As time allowed evolution to do its work, entangling with chemistry, light, and matter, life continued to strengthen itself through evolution as plants, and then insects, and animals became common place in this reality on earth.

Life continued to improve upon itself as humans evolved, with sudden rapid improvements in the human DNA which provide a significant advantage over the animals that lived among us way back then. Life continued to evolve and improve with the passage of time. Life has the ability to create opportunities as time and experience move along.

When something works well enough to prolong survival, it has statistical advantages to reproduce those qualities. Natural mathematics at evolutionary work.

The cosmological spacial dimensions on the earth have provided perfect conditions for life to evolve, and thrive. Earth contains lots of water, plants required minerals (good dirt), abundant sunlight, and correct temperature ranges.

The earth presently houses more than seven million different species of life within its bounty. A living planet earth moved through cycles of temperature, and atmospheric chemistry over time, as it evolved ever on in time. Earth has provided all of life's requirements, even into the present-day technology of humans which required petroleum product to thrive, which are derived from ancient plant and animal remains, through chemistry and time.

Life itself is likened to space, as it is host to many sentient spacial dimensions alike. The matter-based body which carries life, allows additional dimensions to exist as symbiotic hosts within itself, which adds to life's enriched state of conscious observational experiences.

13. Consciousness - #2 Sentient spacial Dimension

Consciousness; is the totality of attitudes, opinions, emotions and sensitiveness held or thought to be held by an individual. Critical awareness. Consciousness is the experience of reality. Without consciousness, reality would not exist for experiencing. Sensations, feelings, thought, insights, consciousness is self-consciousness. Consciousness is thought to be without material, mass or physical form. Consciousness is thought to be without end, but changes form over time. Consciousness contains intent and ability to interact and experience by means of awareness. It is now apparent that human's, animals and plants alike are conscious.

Consciousness fits our criteria of a sentient spacial dimension in that it exists in our universe. Consciousness is different from the cosmological dimensions in that it is aware of itself. Consciousness is by definition to be called a sentient spacial dimension.

Consciousness; has a level of existence, and a group of properties. Consciousness is a fundamental aspect of reality, without which there would be no reality to experience. Consciousness has a scope of magnitude, and a physical quantity which can be measured, as well as space and time can be measured.

Consciousness is the fundamental aspect of reality due to its sentient nature, and self-awareness parameters. Consciousness realizes reality thereby making it the primary sentient dimension. Consciousness entangles with life, and the other cosmological and sentient spacial dimensions, by means of experiences.

Recently a couple of microbiologists on opposite sides of the earth from each other discovered that consciousness was derived by means of an interactive quantum entanglement phenomenon, electro chemical reaction within the microtubules of the brain, in humans and animals.

The microtubules are microscopic conduits which connect brain neurons with one another in web like structures within the brain. Inside the tiny microtubules conduits, energized information carrying electrons become quantum entangled (in more than one place, at a time) while existing in the microtubule, and outside the body simultaneously.

Entangled electrons can exist as anti-matter (positrons or anti-electrons) and matter at the same time. This microtubule entanglement produces an electromagnetic aura around the head and body of humans, animals, and even around plants. This phenomenon (entangled electron within microtubules) is now thought to be the method of attaining consciousness by means of natural life functions.

This energized electrical field around the body, and within the brains microtubules simultaneously, is generated by means of entangled spacial dimensions in symbiotic relationships to each other. More on this later.

A seldom used form of specialized photography called Kirllian photography, illuminates this electrical field around living beings. This quantum entangled electrical field (consciousness) is thought to be a visual aspect of living consciousness.

Consciousness then is the result of entanglement of all spacial dimensions which allow life to become self-aware. As the spacial dimensions evolve to become more complex, it becomes apparent that team work of multiple systems, both sentient, and cosmological (quantum entanglement) is essential for consciousness to exist. Without the material body, and the old dead star produced elements, the living consciousness would not have evolved into the observer of this discussion on string theory, the edge of reality.

Consciousness consists of awareness, and is physically (electrically entangled electrons) constructed of the energized electrons entangled within and around the living body, and its nervous system (Microtubules). Consciousness is the bodily spirit which gives life to the multiple entangled material systems which life uses as its vehicle, species dependent. The consciousness exists in the spacial and sub-spacial dimensions simultaneously, as its energized electrons entangle between the electron and anti-electron states. This is occurring within the spacial and sub-spacial dimensions simultaneously. Consciousness holds within itself the aspects of thought, emotion, and imagination which all entangle within spacial and sub-spacial dimensions simultaneously by their very natures.

Within your consciousness is your; I (personal aspect of consciousness), from where your self-talk is generated within yourself. This I, then observes and reacts to the images and ideas presented (experienced) to it through reality, and the observations of the; I (yourself).

Any conscious debate within the individuals mind implies a dualistic quality of consciousness, which when both are considered as a living within a material body, then creates a dualistic consciousness situation. One aspect of consciousness is the; I, and the other is the conscience, which debates with the; I. Think of the little angle and devil sitting on your shoulders as you decide which course of action to follow.

The body is alive, and the consciousness is a dualistic living entity of the material body by definition alone; "Consciousness is thought to be without mass or form"-by definition.

Body, consciousness, and then a debate with conscience in your head, mathematically adds up to three aspects of the living body, a trinity. Still with me there?

Consciousness through time and evolution historically entangled into matter little by little. As life's physical material structure became more intricate, life and consciousness evolved and gained aspects of reality over time. Description of evolutionary life forms, roughly as follows.

1. <u>Mineral bacteria's</u> – single celled organisms
2. <u>Complex bacteria's</u> – Multi-Cellular organisms - symbiotic cooperation
3. <u>Plants</u> – Nervous system – entangled electrons-multi cellular- symbiotic cooperation - entangled electrons – instinctive behavior
4. <u>Insects</u> – Nervous systems – multi cellular – entangled electrons – symbiotic cooperation – instinctive behavior - communication
5. <u>Animals</u> – Nervous system – entangled electrons-multi cellular- symbiotic cooperation - entangled electrons – instinctive behavior- observation – memory - communication - emotion
6. <u>Humans</u> – Nervous systems - multi cellular – symbiotic cooperation - entangled electrons – observation – memory - thought – learning - emotion – imagination –spirituality - technology – religion
7. <u>Artificial intelligence</u> – Technology - Synthetic electronics - entangled electrons – entertainment
8. <u>Virtual reality</u> – Technology - Synthetic electronics - entangled electrons- limitless realities – entertainment

Is life responsible for the evolution of the reality in which it has been born into? Is it life's purpose to evolve reality into more than it was initially? Consciousness entangles through evolution (time) in a quantum bundles as phases of more and more complex life evolves on planet earth.

Symbiotic relationships are required for life to exist, such as the mitochondria in the cells of all animal life, and the gut bacteria in the stomach of all animal life. Life evolves in fractal increments and then diversifies into many species as a matter of survival probabilities with intelligent evolutionary tactics. Consciousness evolves itself to be more and more entangled with each fractal dimensional leap of living evolution into matters quantum entangled complexity.

Living consciousness continues to deepen its impregnation into reality as time marches forward. Consciousness is entangled within reality and continues to press deeper and deeper into itself, in effort to evolve and improve, its ability to observe and experience that which it is immersed within. Conscious life that is aware of itself, what else would it do? Is the dimension of consciousness knowingly evolving through time, growing more complex and entangled into reality as a matter of intent, of the said sentient spacial dimensional consciousness?

In our string theory discussion of the multi-dimensional reality, consciousness fits into place for the open-minded onlooker.

14. Emotion – #3 Sentient spacial Dimension

Emotion; the sub-parameter of consciousness which involves feelings or sensitivities. Psychological change in thought, cognitive response, in preparation for action. Emotions are involved by observation of stimuli, or reality. Some of the emotions we perceive are love, happiness, joy, jealousy, hatred, lust. Etc.

Strong emotions can elicit extreme electro chemical, and ultimately physical action in animals and humans alike. Emotion can cause uncontrollable physical response to stimulus. Situational interpretation of conscious observation creates emotional stimulation. Emotional stimulation can create physical reaction.

Emotional experiences are among the most intense aspects of living consciousness. Consciousness has the ability to control emotional response, in physical actions, but not so much with respect to mental emotion in response to unexpected stimuli.

Emotional surprise causes electro chemical action within the nervous system, which prompts actions, as defense mechanisms built into the body. Fight or flight responses are triggered in animals and humans as instinctive defense mechanisms, survival tactics of mathematical probability.

Emotion fits the requirements of a spacial dimension as much as time or space does, in that emotions reside within our reality.

Emotions are quantifiable, and contain a group of properties, such as love, joy, etc. Emotion has a level of existence, and is a fundamental aspect of reality. Emotion has a scope of magnitude, and a fundamental measure of physical quantity. Emotion fits all of the requirements to be considered as a spacial dimension for our string theory discussion, in our open-minded perspective on reality. Emotion is one of the more dynamic and impactful sentient spacial dimensions, with respect to having catalytic influences to situations and behavior.

Emotion can be considered to be a reactionary sentient spacial dimension that entangles itself into all other spacial dimensions. It is difficult to gain control over Emotion when consciousness life is surprised; automatic reaction can result. Emotions entangle through chemistry, consciousness, life, and within all of the cosmological dimensions, perhaps, time more than the others when a surprise is involved. Surprises can force consciousness to control emotional response in a very short time, before an automatic response, responds instinctively. New love creates distractions and imaginational experiences which are highly desired by most, experiencing them.

Emotions allow humans and animals to experience a wide variety of dynamic experiences through life. Treasured, and feared are the emotional dynamics we will find ourselves entangled within, from time to time in our lives. This dimensional aspect of reality may be more influential than any others despite its elusive, and uncontrollable nature.

Consciousness being a sentient dimension has developed the emotional sub-dimension, as it expands itself deeper into reality through evolution. Both consciousness and its child, emotion, are well adapted to be dimensional considerations as they are both quantifiable, they both have groups of properties, they have some levels of existence, and they are fundamental units of reality. Emotion qualifies as a sentient spacial dimension of consciousness in our string theory discussion of reality.

15. Imagination – #4 Sentient spacial Dimension

Imagination; is the ability of consciousness to form mental images or concepts which are not real, or present. Such ability the consciousness is used creatively. The ability to confront or cope with reality by using the creative power of the conscious mind. Such as resourcefulness. The ability of the conscious mind to create fantasies, useful in developing new ideas, technical theories, as we are doing now, and problem solving.

Imagination allows for intended diversions from reality for children, and creative adults. Alternative realities can be witnessed in the individual's imagination by means of day dreaming, meditation, and sleeping dreams, in which the sub-conscious mind takes charge of mental priorities by means of intent.

The Penial gland within the brain is thought to activate the mental images associated with imagination, insight and meditative imaging. Many pioneering scientists such as Albert Einstein, Newton, Ramanujan and Tesla used imagination to conduct thought experiments to extrapolate unattainable data, which then allowed science to evolve and grow. Imagination takes place within the sub-spacial dimension, by means of quantum entanglement of consciousness, within the living body.

Many of the imagined images, especially in the engineering field eventually become real product, which were initially conceived through imagination. Even the world's most read religious book says; "If it can be imagined, it can be made by the hands of man". Think about humanity's technology, and think of one product which was not first imagined before coming into realities existence. Necessity is the root of all creation in this world's reality.

Did you ever watch a cat, sitting there staring into space? Is the cat lost within its imagination? The cat seems completely content while in that state of consciousness, and will remain until it needs to do something relevant. Dogs often are seen asleep with their legs in chase mode, as if running after something despite the fact that they are sleeping. Dreaming images and imaginational images are created in the same manner. While dreaming, or meditating is reality, relative to time?

The living consciousness, entangles through imagination into the sub-spacial dimension to form images, in a four-dimensional aspect of mental reality. I know that I dream in color, and hear sound, touch and feel things, smell, taste things, and experience emotional aspects of consciousness while dreaming or imagining. Often times my dreams are so real, that even when I realize I'm dreaming, I find it incredible that the dream seems so realistic, and is an alternative reality for the time it exists. I often wish the dream would have continued indefinitely.

Imagination also fits the qualification parameters to be considered a sentient spacial dimension in our quest to resolve string theory in this edge of reality discussion. Imagination is quantifiable, and has a group of properties. It has a scope of magnitude, and is a fundamental measure of physical quantity. Imagination is a fundamental aspect of reality with respect to conscious life, and experiences. It becomes clear that imagination meets all requirements to be considered a sentient spacial dimension for our string theory discussion.

Imagination directly entangles with all spacial dimensions in our reality thought experiment, if viewed from a positive perspective. Imagination entangles within the living consciousness through means of sub-spacial involvement, which permits multi-dimensional imaging without actual multi-dimensional spacial requirements. Imagination occurs in the negative sub-spacial environment, directly opposite of our visible reality.

Imagination is the result of quantum entangled consciousness energized electrons, being instinctually directed into the alternate reality of conscious intent. If imagination were not able to entangle into sub-space where would the incredible images be, that we see. There is no movie projection screen within our living brains, just electrical wiring, water, and fat, nothing much more.

Imagination allows the living consciousness to create a natural virtual reality within itself in sub-spacial entangled dimension, for self-indulgence, idea formation, creation, daydreaming, child's play.

Imagination can also cause the brain to release endorphins such as dopamine, as a placebo effect within the body to create desired feeling from the imaginationary process, of a self-rewarding phenomenon. The endorphins released in the brain, reveal that imagination is viewed as a reality by the conscious life, due to the power of the emotional content of the imagination. Imagination entangles deeply within the living consciousness, and emotional dimensions attempting to convince the living body that its imaginary contents are real. This imaginational placebo effect is currently being employed as a medical practice in many places around our world.

In stressful time a child may gravitate into an imaginary situation to escape the reality it fears, at any given moment. Adults may take refuge in drugs or alcohol to achieve the escape that the child naturally uses imagination to sub-consciously control. Imagination is being used in medical circles with respect to placebo drugs which can be as useful as, or even better than prescription drug to alleviate major health issues.

Presently certain doctors are allowing their patients to design their own placebo pills, in an effort to cure unresolvable health problems, with a marked increase in success rates. The patient is actually aware that the designed pill is a placebo, yet cure rate results are better than using the prescription medications for many of these patients. The placebo effect utilizes the power of the living consciousness's imagination to take control of body functioning, and uses positive thinking, and faith to allow the body to cure itself.

Imagination is a very strong sentient spacial dimension, in that it allows creativity, creation, healing, and gives a positive meaning to life. It is capable of giving great pleasure, or incredible fear, it is dynamic, and useful to every living being that is lucky enough to experience it.

16. Observation – #5 Sentient spacial Dimension

Observation; the act of viewing and assessing what is being viewed. The act of nothing, while recording something. The act of watching. Applying attention to a subjects, event or situations. The act of scientific experimentation when testing for a result. That to observe an event, is to experience the mentioned event.

Quantum mechanics dictates that experimental outcome is determined by the method of relative observation. Relativity states that observation from different positions results in different relative observational perspectives, and experimental results. In other words, the way we observe, determines the way that we witness.

Observation, an exercised extension of consciousness, fits into the required criteria of a spacial dimension, in that the observation takes place within the universe or reality, which covers the spacial aspect of our new way of looking at string theory. You are observing this discussion now, in an observational spacial dimension different from the observation that I am writing it from, or from a different perspective.

Observation; is quantifiable, and has a group of properties; such as experimental parameters, and perspective points of view. Observation has a level of existence, and is a fundamental unit of reality; by observation does reality exist. Observation has a scope of magnitude; example macro or micro. Observation has a fundamental measure of physical quantity. Observation is a sentient spacial dimension, and meets the defined requirements to assist with respect to string theory actualization. Open minds create improved observational perspectives of reality!

Observation entangles specific spacial dimensions depending on the subject being observed, and the perspective of the observation; relativity. Observation entangles directly with consciousness, emotion, imagination, life, light, matter, time, space, gravity, temperature, force, chemistry, communication, etc.

Observation occurs when consciousness directs awareness into focus with respect to a specific situation of interest. Observation is required for communication in the conscious act of listening, imagining or learning.

In a thought experiment; imagine the human eyes to be able see reality through the entire electromagnetic spectrum, rather than just visible light. You would see me with x-ray, infrared, and gamma wave lengths. You would see me as a glowing light creature, like an angel, but also with all of my bones showing through like a skeleton. The entire electromagnetic spectrum would be observed some of which would be reflecting, others passing through me, and some just illuminating me. The observation would be relative to the observational parameters, like ultra-vision.

If our observations of reality showed everything, in every electromagnetic wavelength, the world would be very confusing to say the least. After all, in reality all matter consists of hundreds of thousands of times more space than solid materials, on the sub-atomic scales of observation.

Quantum mechanics and relativity theories dictated mathematically that all scientific experimentation outcome, is dictated through means of observation, relative to the observer. The Holographic principle, Bells theorem, Quantum mechanics, Physics 101, all dictate the same thing, so what is reality, really? What are you observing to be reality at present? Is the edge of reality within, or without.

Observational relativity is a required sentient spacial dimension to verify consciousness, imagination and emotion in reality. Combining the cosmological and sentient dimensions is making the String Theory look more and more plausible, the magic eye picture gains focus, as we continue to allow our thoughts to take on a new perspective. The open mind absorbs ideas like a dry sponge, while our discussion of string theory's edge of reality parameters come closer to full focus in your minds eye.

17. Communication - #6 Sentient spacial Dimension

Communication; the exchange of ideas, message, or information as by speech, signals, writing, etc. A system for sending and receiving messages. Communication, devices include body language, voice, pen and paper, telegraph, telephone, email, texting, etc. Conscious awareness allows intentional communication between like species with respect to all sentient life forms known. Cross communication between species is extremely rare as a natural protective devise, animals, plants and insects utilize different forms and levels of communication which are almost always species specific. Humans have used technology to diversify communications mediums, and platforms in a conscious effort to evolve.

Communication fits our criteria as a sentient spacial dimension as we open our minds to a new way of looking at reality, in our quest to unfold string theories mysterious way of being. Communication does exist in our universe, qualifying it as a spacial dimension.

Communication; has a level of existence, and is quantifiable. It has a scope of magnitude, a group of properties, and is a fundamental aspect of reality. Communication has a fundamental measure of physical quantity. The dictionary definition agrees. As stated communication is a solid player in the spacial dimensions required for string theory mathematics to work out in a proof, which can verify the existence of it, in itself.

Communications of a fractal and quantum level occur throughout all living species, by means of DNA driven auto response electro chemical signals which automate body organs of a material nature, which are the mechanical devices of a body.

Just as sub-space exists to support imagination, and consciousness, sub-consciousness exists to support life functions for bodies to live. Matter and anti-matter balance each other in reality just as do consciousness and sub-consciousness, space and sub-space.

Communications can trigger chemical reactions through imagination with respect to placebo phenomenon or observational, and emotional conscious awareness or beliefs, (faith).

Communications entangled into early life by means of bio-chemical signals within multi-celled life forms. These electro signals were then used as nervous systems and evolved in animals and insects. Insects then communicated with audio signals, and body language, then soon after all sentient life followed suit. Technology entangled with communication as earthly evolution continued.

Communication at the basic level is mathematics written media. Extraterrestrial intelligence would likely employ a mathematical statement of information, as a first contact to communicate with humans on earth. Crop circles designed in the form of fractal patterns or Mandelbrot sets which could determine the reader's intelligence level, by the response. This may have already occurred in many places around the world.

Communication accuracy is imperative to cross communicate between species. The higher intelligent species would be responsible to communicate in a manner to which the lesser intelligent species would be able to understand and respond. Arrogance of the lesser intelligent species could inhibit the actual communication, and by means of ignorant arrogance, prevent an intelligent response. Think about asking your pet for a response, and how you communicate your intent.

It may be that higher intelligent species have attempted to openly communicate with humans, but due to many factors of ignorance, or arrogance, the humans have been oblivious, or avoided such contact. From ancient religious scripts to crop circle humans have mounting evidence that the universe is teaming with intelligent life forms, more advanced than ourselves. The sheer number of stars systems in the visible universe alone is incomprehensible. The odds of intelligent life existing beyond earth is overwhelming.

Intelligent thoughtful communications may improve the odds of developing a good relationship with outside extraterrestrial life forms in our future. Too bad we can't do just that within our own governmental circles on earth.

18. *Memory - #7 Sentient spacial Dimension*

Memory; is the mental faculty of retaining and storing past experiences. Persistent modification of behavior resulting of past experiences. Capacity for retaining information, engram of mind. Memory fits into the new way of thinking about spacial dimensions for string theory. It exists in our physical universe.

Memory is quantifiable, it exists, and is a fundamental aspect, or unit of reality, without which we would not likely remember anything about reality any ways. It has a level of existence, and has a group of properties. Memories can be provoked by certain songs, smells, sights, or any number of stimuli. Memory has a measurable physical quantity, and a scope of magnitude, thereby qualifying it as a spacial dimension for our string theory discussion.

Memory indirectly entangles within all of the spacial dimensions, and is required for intelligence to exist. Life, observation, communication, thinking, behaving, and even imagining, would have little value without a memory of them to enjoy, or beware of in the future.

Our string theory quest would have little meaning without the memories of the factors considered to achieve its validity. Remembering who we are seems like a trivial effort, until the individual becomes afflicted with dementia, and cannot remember anything. Memory has much to do with individuality. String theory would have little meaning whether right, wrong, or just a wild guess to someone without memory capacity.

Memory gives rise to evolution, through means of improvements of all tasks, and tool implements utilized in evolution itself. Memories can be treasured, family activities, loved ones in embrace. Memories can prevent dangerous behavior, and accident avoidance. Remembering what not to do can save a life. Simply remembering what not to eat allowed humans to evolve, instead of poisoning themselves out of existence. Scientist conducting experiment must remember protocol, and observational perspectives to proceed successfully.

Remembering your wife's birthday, and anniversary will help to avoid and reduce future bad days of married men around the world. Memory fits all criteria for sentient spacial dimensional consideration due to the fore mentioned.

19. Thinking – #8 Sentient spacial Dimension

Thinking; is to have or to formulate in the conscious mind. A way of reasoning. Marked by the ability to think. To reason about something. To ponder. To judge or regard. To believe or suppose. To devise or invent. To bring into a mental state by preoccupation. To reason by deduction. To decide, or to decide against after considering. To consider. Determining which action to pursue after consideration.

Understanding foundational considerations and accessible parameters for solving problems.

Does thinking fall into our spacial dimensional category? Thinking occurs in the physical universe. Thinking is quantifiable, and it has a group of properties. Thinking has a level of existence, you're thinking about it right now, as you read this. Thinking is a fundamental unit of reality which would not be recognized without itself. Only a thinking person would realize that fact. Thinking has a scope of magnitude, and a measure of physical quantity. Thinking requires conscious intent to indulge consciousness into it state of being. Thinking is quantifiable.

Thinking directly entangles with consciousness, emotion, imagination, memory, life and learning, as well as observation. Thinking can indirectly entangle with all other spacial dimensions, in which we can discuss.

Thinking guides and directs humanities evolution with respect to technology, ethical and moral decisions, and ultimate directions. Conscious thinking, logically (hypothetically) should keep humanity on track to avoid species self-destruction. Thinking should keep humanity on a safe and prosperous evolutionary, technological path (hypothetically).

Practical thinking can be diverted, or distracted by self-indulgence, rather than logic when desires fed by greed are not tempered, or recognized. Greed is capable of driving emotional content into dangerous aspects of reality. Thinking allows determination of direction with respect to evolution, and technologies. Progress determines if thinking was executed for the better, or for the worse, in the long run. Perspective then becomes the important aspect of thinking, with respect to outcome of thinking projects intentual executions. Perspective in thought is relative to objective of behavior.

Thinking engages the consciousness with respect to the life quality of any individual's situation, what's in it for me, syndrome. I can get a lot of money by doing this or that, but what is the reaction of me doing this or that? Will my benefit, hurt another, or cause environmental damage. Greed and ignorance are shortcomings of limited thinking, or closed-minded individuals, and seem to drive consumerism in most of the world today.

Thinking can entangle with the imagination to provide unavailable situations in the mind's eye, or sub-spacial dimensions of consciousness. Thinking experiments have allowed creative individuals to conceive the impossible outcomes, with insight (thinking combined with imagination).

Many individuals believe that insightful thinking, and some forms of imaginative thought are the result of direct entanglement with the Akashic Records, (sub-spacial dimension) black hole event horizons, information storage devise.

Information paradox theory states that all information entering into the event horizon of a black hole is stored in its time trap, for later extraction. Think about using thought as a spacial dimension as we continue our journey to unravel the mysteries of string theory, at the edge of reality.

Thinking can give imagination direction, but it cannot lead it to conclusions. Imagination is within the consciousness, while thinking directs the consciousness, with considerations of this or that, depending on something else. Many parameters can be involved in a simple thinking process, or experiment. Whereas the imagination carries out the fantasy of the pondering intentional foundation of the individual. Thinking directs the intent, while pondering or considering the facts of the matter at hand.

20. Spirituality - #9 Sentient spacial Dimension

Spirituality; according to the dictionary is to be concerned with the soul (consciousness). Concerned with affecting the soul. Relating to God. The belief that the dead communicate with the living. A philosophy emphasizing spiritual, rather than material. A refined mind. So according to the dictionary a refined mind is a spiritual mind.

Spirituality is a consciousness, sentient spacial dimension naturally occurring in humans since, and before recorded history and is entangled within all hominid societies worldwide. The naturally occurring belief in a higher intelligence, or creator whom is to be respected and worshiped. Spiritual individuals believe without reservation that bodily death is only a passing from one state of consciousness to another state of consciousness. The dictionary states that consciousness is thought to be without end.

Spirituality fits into the parameters of a spacial dimension for string theory consideration. Spirituality is quantifiable, either you are, or you are not. At least ninety five percent of human's report being of a spiritual nature worldwide. Spirituality has a group of properties, and has a level of existence. It is a fundamental aspect of reality, and has a scope of magnitude. Spirituality meets all definitional requirements for our string theory discussion.

Through spirituality, the human race has separated into various religious sects in an effort to amplify, and pursue the spiritual yearning within themselves. Spirituality has entangled through communication, observation, emotions, imagination, thinking, learning, and memory as conscious living beings, to embrace spirituality as a sentient spacial dimension by definition.

Spirituality governs conscious life individuals to behave in a constructive and respectful manner amongst themselves, thereby safeguarding living existence for all species on the planet. Spirituality implies moral and ethical entanglement parameters which are deduced from mathematics (logic), and thinking skill; if I kill too many animals for my food needs, my food supply will soon be extinguished. Even the lowly animal predators abide by these rules of conduct.

It is only certain members of the human species whom greed has taken hold of, and are found to be outside of spiritual, ethical, moral, logical, and intelligent conduct boundaries of true spirituality.

An example of this is the extinction of the wild Buffalo on the Great Plains in America. Buffalo were exterminated for their hides, and mercilessly hunted until none remained. The buffalo meat was discarded as unnecessary for commerce or food, as the species was eradicated. The Buffalo hides were needed for money, but greed prevented many humans from thinking and using logic, to extend the cash flow at the expense of short term gains. These individuals allowed greed to overtake spirituality and thought.

It is ultimately spirituality which drive scientific, astronomical, and biological research to find truth about reality, and the existence of God, through mathematics, observations, memory, imagination, emotion, communications, thought, and behaviors. All of the spacial dimensions entangle in an attempt to evolve, improve and progress onward with respect to intelligence, and growth through their own technology exploitation. Spirituality is an experience in which hope, is entangled with imagination and thought, understanding that our living consciousness is more than just the life in our own bodies here on earth today.

Spirituality is a sentient spacial dimension in our string theory discussion, which aids in our future behavior, as a species on the earth. It drives humanity to find answers to long asked questions, and to keep to a constructive path in doing so. Spirituality lays clear lines in the sand of ethical and moral conduct, which require little thought to analyze correctly.

21. Learning - #10 Sentient spacial Dimension

Learning; is to gain or acquire knowledge. Comprehension of study or observation to fix in the mind. Committing to memory to be educated. Acquired skills, wisdom or knowledge. Application of memorized knowledge to specific task related skill execution. Learning to read is required to understand and enjoy books. Learning to ride a bicycle is required for most children. Learning to cook, allows for more satisfying meals. Learning what not to do, is likely the most important learning humans can undertake, to avoid getting into trouble. A deer crossing the road either learns to look for traffic, or dies in its ignorance by crossing a busy section of roadway. A fawn learns not to cross the road in traffic, after experiencing the aforementioned accident, it learns by observing.

Learning fits into our string theory spacial dimension requirement. Learning is quantifiable, and has a scope of magnitude. Learning is a fundamental aspect of reality, and has a group of properties. Learning has a fundamental measure of physical quantity, like a test score. Learning is a willful act of consciousness, thought, and observation, through memory.

Humanity's ability to learn is greater than any other species on the planet, and has allowed humans to beget technology, and reap the benefits and downfalls of its existence. As the learning aspect of life continues to evolve, humanity grows closer and closer to attaining sciences number one goal. To understand and explain reality in a unified field theory. Solving string theory will bring humanity one step closer to this lofty goal.

Learning directly entangles with consciousness, observation, thought, imagination, life, memory, matter, time, space, gravity, etc., you get the idea. Humanity has an unassailable thirst to learn more, and more about everything it can. Its imagination drives humanities intelligence to push the boundaries even further than logical mathematics dictate possible. Learning allows humans to find new mathematical solutions to make imaginary thought into reality, with communications, and technologies.

Learning fits into the sentient spacial dimensional category and may prove to be either the most important parameter of reality, or the most dangerous, depending on its deterministic usage in the future with respect to applied technologies potential and executions.

By means of learning humanity has been able to create several synthetic dimensions as byproducts of technology and behavior. Humans utilize technology, and learning in many ways, some of which are potentially dangerous, and some helpful for humanity. By combining all that humanity is aware of, learning should (logically) be employed to safeguard the future of earth (our home) and humanity alike. The present threat of global warming exposes the contrary as being factual, instead of the logical contrary being true. Confusion to me and you to, that humanity would risk everything for nothing.

What is it that humanity is doing with all that it has learned, hoarding money and creating war, to what ends?

22. DNA - #11 Sentient spacial Dimension or #1 Synthetic spacial Dimension

DNA; is the odd spacial dimension in our string theory discussion, as it seems to be synthetic in composition, and complexity, and sentient in functionality at the same time. DNA is the operating system for all life on this planet. It is an electro-chemical operational system which is far beyond human technological understanding. Teams of scientist have studied to understand its complexities for decades without complete success.

Each DNA stand within every cell in living tissue contains more than thirty million chemical codes, or instructions which provide the operating system for life in matter as we understand it today. Like electricity, gravity, and even lightning, humans can use it, but cannot explain it. DNA can be used as a tool, to enhance most parameters of a living body in many ways. Technology allows individual DNA strands to be spliced, into itself to correct mistakes in living cells. CRISPER technology is in its infancy, but looks promising in its seemly endless potential with respect to enhancing DNA shortcomings in living things.

DNA is by definition; Deoxyribonucleic acid; a polymeric chromosomal constituent of living cell nuclei, having two long chains of alternating phosphate, and deoxyribose units twisted into a double helix, and joined ladder like by hydrogen bonds between the complimentary bases, Adenine and Thymine or Cytosine and Guanine, each of which projects towards the helix from one of the strands where it is bonded in a sequence that determines individual heredity characteristics, species, life span and long term health conditions to say the least.

DNA is so complex that the scientist who discovered it, stated that it could not have evolved naturally, therefore must be the result of intelligent design beyond human intellectual capacity.

DNA does fit the criteria for a (synthetic) spacial dimension in our open-minded discussion of string theory parameters, as we strive to think in with open minds, from fresh perspectives, allowing the magic eye picture to become clearer to our string theory vision of reality.

DNA; has a level of existence, and is quantifiable, DNA has a set of properties. DNA is a fundamental unit of reality. DNA has a scope of magnitude, and a fundamental measure of physical quantity. DNA has a number of independent parameters required to specify a quantifiable aspect of reality. DNA meets the criteria for a spacial dimension in our string theory discussion.

Without DNA there would be no life, no string theory discussion, no you or me. However DNA became real (evolution or creation), it allows life to exist, and evolve by means of temporal entanglement of matter, chemistry, and space-time. DNA commands individual cells to specialize in exact numbers to grow a conscious living being of any of the seven million species on earth, with only minor differences between any two species, less than 5%. It does this with incredible success rates, and accuracy factors.

DNA remains the most mysterious spacial dimension in our reality to present day time. It is possible that we will discover its origins in the distant future, as technology and intelligence evolve. DNA is an information storage system which my already contain its origins. Future technology may allow the secrets of DNA to be learned by humans.

Considering the number of habitable planets in the actual universe, and the probability that intelligent life does exist outside of human awareness, DNA could be accounted for as seeded into our planetary habitation with intent by distant neighbors of some intelligent species. DNA is adaptable, and being manipulatable in nature. Probability wise I'm leaning to the side of DNA being intelligently designed, rather than having evolved naturally. If DNA is really a sentient dimension, then it would be number eleven on that chart. You can make up your own mind on that point. DNA may be a synthetic dimension for all we know, time may tell us more about that.

DNA technology is allowing humanity to enhance many living species in an effort to improve specific parameters of the living condition with marked success. As living consciousness strives to evolve the perfect human body, will we finally understand the DNA molecule and its actual purpose? Will human tampering with this spacial dimension improve our existence, or hamper it with unexpected side effects from its manipulations. Many individuals think that using DNA to manipulate living conscious beings is a moral, and ethical travesty. Some individuals think that humans do not have the right to play God with the DNA technology.

DNA technology has the potential to extend the life span of humans by a factor of ten or more. This would lead to numerous considerations to avoid overpopulation, long term boredom, 500-year marriage partners, livelihood factors, and other important results of this potential technology.

Thinking on these matters, without the greed factors may help to avoid unforeseen problems arising from such technological efforts in the future. As humans evolve, their behavior will dictate the outcome of their choices with respect to technology, and environmental factors which humans rely upon for basic survival.

23. *Behavior - #2 Synthetic spacial Dimension*

Behavior; the manner in which one behaves. One's actions under specific circumstances. The manner in which one operates. Behavioral psycho physics; psychology with respect to measuring sensory capacities within living animals. Behaviorism, observable and quantifiable aspects of behavior, or manner in which one operates or acts. Behave, to act, react, function, or perform in a specific way. To conduct oneself.

Behavior meets the dictionary's definitional requirements of a synthetic spacial dimension. Behavior is quantifiable, and has a group of properties. Behavior is a fundamental unit, or aspect of reality, and has a level of existence. Behavior has a group of properties, and a scope of magnitude. Behavior is what conscious living being do. Behavior is what defines individuals, what and who they are.

Behavior is perhaps the most important spacial dimension in reality with respect to living beings who dwell in the physical universe. People live to do things, talked to each other, and behave. Humans interact, or behave. Behavior is the way in which we interact with each other in society. Behavior defines our individual personalities, and allows predictable reactions within given situations. Behavior is where free will, and achievement enter into the human, and animal equation.

Behavior is the physical act such as working, playing, fighting, or loving, and therefore is a synthetic spacial dimension. Behavior such as thinking, or anger and imagination, are sub-spacial behaviors, which initially occur only in the mind. Spacial and sub-spacial behaviors allows conscious life to entangle with itself within the sting theory reality. Without behavior, (interaction) why live? Behavior gives distinction to individual conscious life forms. Constructive or destructive, helpful or unhelpful, behaviors have a direct impact on physical reality, with respect to social, and planetary progress and even evolution. Behavior is the end game to realities future.

Behavior can lead to, and also prevent wars between groups of individuals, or governing countries. Behavior can lead to destructive technologies, or beneficial technologies. Behavior comes down to the choice that conscious living individuals, or groups choose to make.

Behavior is the synthetic spacial dimension which will determine humanities future experiences, observations, and fate. Behavior is an individual choice, one can love, one can hate. The list of potential behaviors in unlimited. Thought comes into play at the edge of reality.

24. Religion - #3 Synthetic spacial Dimension

Religion; belief in, or reverence for a supernatural power accepted as the creator, and governor of the universe. The conscious attitude of one who recognizes the existence of a superhuman intelligence. An objective pursued with reverence or conscientious devotion, spiritualism is religious and believes that the living can communicate with the dead though a medium. A philosophy doctrine emphasizing the conscious spirit rather than the material. Each separate religion has specific guidelines, and religious ceremonies to which its followers respect and practice. Religion is the end result of spiritualism. Religion has a very specific story of god, and gods desires for humanity. A specific spiritual belief system for its cult followers, with rules and regulation of conduct.

Religion fits into the string theory parameters for a synthetic spacial dimension. It is a specific chosen behavioral aspect of spirituality, as consciousness is to life.

Religion is a specific belief that god wants humanity to follow certain rules of conduct, and punishes those who do not comply. Religions have duties for compliance, such as prayers, and fasting ceremonies, and even currency collection requirements for its participants. Religions have governmental rankings for its individuals, and separate governing from following.

Spirituality does not impose rules of conduct with respect to consequences, and membership. Spirituality is a natural understanding that life does not end at death, and that god is running the universe, naturally.

Religion fits into the synthetic spacial dimensional parameters as it has a level of existence, and a scope of magnitude, and is a fundamental unit of reality. Religion has a group of properties, and a fundamental measure of physical quantity, as much as space or time do. Religion exists in the physical universe, and attempts to explain its own existence, as it is a synthetic spacial dimension which was created by conscious living humans.

Religion entangles with consciousness, emotion, imagination, thinking, observation, learning, memory, life, time, space, and all of the other spacial dimensions. Religion defies science as being able to explain reality, in terms of evolution, theories, and time frames. Religion maintains that god created all of reality, and that science is exhaustive in its evolution of errors. Regardless of specific religions accuracy, it is a synthetic spacial dimension created by the living, thinking, and consciousness of humanity.

Religion and science seem to be on track to agree with each other in many ways as scientific discoveries continue to be published. Religion also is now coming to give credit to scientists for proving, and improving on aspects of reality such as the actual age of the universe, and also maintain that some of the religious historical doctrine was written to give estimated, and non-literal descriptions of certain occurrences. If you can't beat em join em.

The entanglement between man's belief in god, and science continues to grow with time. Aspects of reality such as the complexity of the DNA molecule continue to defy scientific reason. The amazing diversity of life on this planet with more than seven million species, defy absolute evolutionary plausibility also.

It is written in religious texts that "man is created in Gods image". This can be interpreted in a couple of ways. I interpret that statement to read that God is dreaming up this reality, in God's own mind. Friends of mine have also interpreted that statement to mean that either God has given man some of his attributes, like emotions; or that we look like God on a different size scale. I'm sure there are other interpretations too. We are created in Gods image out there, which can be made to sound plausible too. In this discussion we are determining if religion is a synthetic spacial dimension, and it has met all required criteria to be considered for such.

String theory may in fact allow a better understanding of the reality of God, in a way that more humans can comprehend, than the mysterious religious texts, vague descriptions. A better understanding of God would seem to be a good thing for anyone religious individual reading this discussion. After all the ultimate goal of science is to explain reality in a provable, and plausible mannerism, with mathematical proofs to back up the statements. An accurate description of reality which explains god in a plausible manner could only benefit humanity.

Religion contains moral and ethical parameters which are meant to guide human behavior in a non-violent, non-destructive manner. Religion dictates that humanity conduct itself in a peaceful manner, to ensure harmony, and growing congregations worldwide. Religions use the threat of afterlife conditions to reinforce their religious doctrine, and human behavioral guidelines. A destructive life according to most religions will result in a miserable afterlife. A constructive and helpful life will result in a good afterlife. Most religions dictate that each individual conscious life's (persons) behavior, will find fair judgment from God, for it, and is the actual will of God.

If our best mathematicians are able to provide proofs for string theory, humanity might have a better understanding of God, and Gods intent than previously. A better understanding of God could only benefit humanity. That is the goal of pure science, to explain everything in reality, for mutual benefit of all.

25. Technology - #4 Synthetic spacial Dimension

Technology; is the body of evolving knowledge available to a civilization that is of use in fashioning implements. Practicing manual arts, and skills, and extracting, or collecting materials. The whole body of methods and materials use to achieve such objectives. The application of science to create and utilize new and improved methods and products. The means by which better tools, products, and methods are attained. The goal of technology is to make a better life for humans.

Technology is quantifiable, from the invention of the wheel, to DNA alterations within many different life forms. Technology is a fundamental aspect of our reality, as it continues to evolve, and attempt to make human lives easier to manage. Technology has a group of properties, and a scope of magnitude. It has a fundamental unit of measure, as it impregnates itself deeper, and deeper into humanities reality. One could even say that humans are becoming enslaved to technology in present day times. Humans rush to repair their technological devices as soon as they manage to break down, prioritizing repair at almost all cost. Humans even depend on technology, try going without your smart phone, television for a week, if you disagree. How about that credit card?

Technology fits into the parameters of a synthetic spacial dimension. It exists in the universe, verifying it is a spacial dimension as much as time is, in our new way of thinking, with open minds, which is leading to the reality of string theory, to describe all that we experience in a comprehensive and practical manner. As we continue to resolve the parameter requirements for string theory's multi-dimensional reality, the magic eye picture begins to unveil itself in layers to our new perspectives. Like the squiggly lines on a (magic eye) page, once observed in the way they were designed to be observed. Once the observational focus is refined, the true picture of reality becomes clear to the conscious living observer.

Initially technology was supposed to allow humans to spend less time each day performing chores, and maintenance tasks. Many present assessments of this premise have determined a shortfall with respect to technology easing the work burden on humanity. Medical, engineering, and processing technologies have greatly reduced manpower requirements, as well as internet sales to reduce travel expenses, and shopping time. War machines have allowed more efficient methods of killing strangers at the same time.

Technology is evolving at exponential rates in most fields at present. It is becoming impossible to keep pace with technology in any one field of study, while all fields continue to grow at this rate, leaving humanity at technologies whim. Poor planning and execution (behavior) of new technologies creates long term risk for humanity, and even the entire planet in some cases. Global warming is one of those situations in which humanity must exercise caution, with the risk being so great. A good question is, will humanities technology eradicate the entire race, along with all living species on the planet, through means of ignorance and greed?

It will be an astonishing accomplishment to realize the components of reality (string theory) by means of technology, logical deduction, mathematics, and consciousness. It would also imply intelligent application of assets in an imaginative conscious reality of self-discovery and interconnected humanitarian self-awareness, which would be a credit to our creator God, for a job well done. We would still have to accomplish the task before destroying ourselves with ignorance. Two sides of one world, constructive, and destructive.

More impressive still is the idea that humanity is in a position to improve its own reality, including humanity itself, with respect to DNA manipulation skills being applied presently (CRISPER). The WEBB telescope will be able to search for intelligent life signs at greater distances that ever dreamed. Cleaner energy systems development to reduce carbon foot print of humanities technology also are steps in the right direction.

Technology entangles with all other spacial dimensions in a direct mannerism, in this reality of multi-dimensional string theory. Technology is changing the human condition through entanglement within Biology, Physics, Electronics, Hydraulics, Communications equipment, Automobiles, computers, the web, Dick Tracy style watches, etc.

It is said in the religious text that "anything that man can imagine, man can create!" We are living that truth presently. Let's imagine a good future for all species on the planet earth, shall we.

26. Currency - #5 Synthetic spacial Dimension

Money; used as a medium for exchange. Generally accepted medium of exchange in commerce. Currency replaced bartering for trade and economic exchange centuries ago in most of the world. Currency is created in mathematically compatible units of tender. Currency is unique to humans, and again unique within each separate governing body, and is usually country specific.

Currency is recognized worldwide despite countless varieties, and constantly variable exchange rates between the varieties, which are ratio dependent on numerous factors. Currency, is possibly the most important worldwide asset of humanity. Currency is used by humans to obtain material things. Currency is used to judge human social status in most of the world. The more currency you obtain, the more valuable and important you become as an individual, in this consumerism based society.

Currency fits into our criteria required to be deemed a synthetic spacial dimension, in that it exists in the universe. Currency is the first of several synthetic spacial dimensions which is a physically man-made commodity in itself.

Currency is quantifiable, and has a group of properties, it has a level of existence, and is now a fundamental unit of reality. Currency has a scope of magnitude, and a fundamental measure of physical quantity. Currency although synthetic, fulfills all dimensional requirements to be considered as a spacial dimension, in our quest to resolve string theory with open minded thinking, and a fresh perspective on said thinking experimentation. We are moving into the edge of reality within this discussion of string theory.

A lack of, or excessive amounts of currency, can and usually does alter conscious perspective of the individual directly involved, and often creates emotional distress, from an amplified perceptual image of the consciousness or self within itself. Conscious thinking of currency situations can cause emotional, and imaginary desires, which amplify actual situational awareness in distortional ways.

Currency represents wealth in individuals, and countries, and is usually the root cause of wars between countries on planet earth. Currency is a powerful and influential synthetic spacial dimension, as it enslaves individuals and countries to its collective nature. Mismanagement of currency usually results in emotional and financial crisis for individuals, and counties alike.

Currency has transformed the primitive natural world reality, into a complex technological consumerism based world reality. Presently individual human worth is now systematically determined by the amount of currency the individual commands. Credit ratings even determine bank loan interest rates. Humanity is now dependent on currency for its survival, as it has become dependent on technology as the foundation of life in society. Humanity wages wars over currency and the acquisition of properties and material assets, in an effort to increase net worth values of themselves, and their taxed citizens.

Humanities reality is now caught like a caged animal, living in our technology based society, which relies on consumerism to exist. Ethical and moral behavior (spirituality) seem to take a back seat when currency is at risk with respect to individuals, or any groups involved. Lives and nations are laid to ruin over currency disputes. Theft is fueled by the desire to obtain currency without working for it. Currency causes unbalance in humanities moral and ethical reality, which also outpours into our planet earths reality, with respect to environmental contamination issues at stake currently (global warming, and pollution issues).

Humanities creation of currency has amplified desire in humans which then amplifies our natural hoarding instincts, which entangles into greed, which arguably is the major contributor to our realities most potentially dangerous situations. With the assistance of currency, humanity can choose to solve major planetary, and humanitarian issues, or just self-indulge in personal desire. Governmental politics and hypocrisy will likely decide humanities fate as a species, by continuing to utilize currency in the ongoing aquirering of tools of war and destruction. The question is, will any documented evidence survive humanities demise, if that is the fate that awaits?

Stock market prices determine investment currency strategies, despite amplified, deceitful reporting methods of commission driven companies. With public retirement plans at stake, consumers invest according to amplified, and deceitful methods, which can destroy the futures of helpful investors.

Morals and ethics are required in business regulations of compliance, but are rarely upheld, at the expense of profits or a sale. Technology has provided unexpected advances in humanities quality of life, as currency continues to amplify humanities need to deceive one another in the name of getting richer.

Greed has been spawned, and evolved into a monster, by the creation of the synthetic spacial dimension of currency. Greed can be said to be the root cause of human suffering, and disparities.

27. *Artificial Intelligence - #6 Synthetic spacial Dimension*

Artificial intelligence; is machine, programed to imitate human intelligence functions, characteristics or parameters of human intellect selected for use in machine which acts like a thinking human, rather than a human tool. A tool comprised of evolving technology which can make choices based upon input, and situational factors to replace humans in technical situations, without advanced programing to a specific task. A thinking machines. Research in methods of programing designed to supplement human intelligence abilities. A portion of humanity, worries that future thinking machines (Artificial Intelligence) may think to eliminate humanity, instead of being enslaved and controlled by it!

Artificial Intelligence fits the criteria of a synthetic spacial dimension by definition. Artificial Intelligence is quantifiable, is now a becoming fundamental unit of reality. It has a group of properties, and a level of existence, and a scope of magnitude. Artificial intelligence has a fundamental measure of physical quantity. It exists in our spacial universe, and thereby meets all of the dictionary requirements of a synthetic spacial dimension for our string theory discussion of reality.

Artificial Intelligence is a logical phase of technical evolution. Chemistry and life slowly entangled to develop human intelligence, with imagination, thought, memory, and so on. Technology then was developed, and eventually evolved until the Artificial Intelligence was inevitable, as a natural progression of technology, in other words it was mathematically (logically) in natural progression or evolution of an intelligent species.

The logical question concerning Artificial Intelligence is how intelligent will it have to become, in order to realize that humans are not superior to it. Then what will Artificial Intelligence to with that intelligent information. Will Artificial Intelligence decide that the humans whom are destroying the planet earth, despite the fact that over seven million other living species share the planet, and are being ignored; must be stopped? Will the Artificial Intelligence decide that the needs of the many (species) outweigh the needs of the few; (Humans)? Will the artificial Intelligence have the means to carry out such a logical extermination procedure? Will the Artificial Intelligence be smart enough to convince humanity to change direction with respect to use of technology?

Human technology has created weapons of mass destruction, in several formats, which could be used against itself by an Artificial Intelligence, if sufficient precautions were not in place to prevent such an occurrence. Are humans capable of foreseeing all possible contingencies with respect to this plausible future self-defeating, self-created situation?

Even more plausible is Artificial intelligence creating a financial disaster (currency exchange rates) within the financial parameters of reality, ex. Stock market crash. One synthetic dimension (artificial Intelligence) using another as a tool (currency) with intent, against humanity.

Artificial Intelligence will entangle with all spacial dimensions in our near future, as most technologies continue to grow at exponential rates. Can humanity control the technology level with respect to artificial Intelligence's evolutionary growth and development, or will greed and ambition to develop the most advanced Artificial Intelligent machine (win the contest) be the end of humanity, due to its reactionary consequences?

What is the purpose of imitating human thought (Artificial Intelligence)? Living consciousness has thought abilities, and is given achievement rewards for using it internally, (dopamine). Is the end game of artificial intelligence to remove thinking from humanity?

If not, then why develop it in the first place. Are you still thinking about the edge of reality, with me?

29. *Virtual Reality - #7 Synthetic spacial Dimension*

Virtual Reality; is a computer simulation of a real or imaginary situational background, or scenery that enables computer user to perform operations on the simulated system, and allows real time controlled interactions on a viewable platform. The computer user interacts directly via controls with the virtual reality system. Virtual Reality is created through the advancement of technology. It is a human creation which imitates imaginational abilities in a controlled imaginary environment. The conscious experience of a virtual reality system is a synthetic imaginational experience, viewed by means of a mask and sound system.

Virtual Reality is the most recent technological synthetic spacial dimensional consideration in reality. Virtual reality is the latest human achievement which combines all of technologies, and imaginationary aspects of living consciousness in a creative manner to provide entertainment for the human observer of it. Unlike Artificial Intelligence, Virtual Reality has recreational value, without the risk of self-annihilation to the human species. It is a form of entertainment for living consciousness observation to be experienced.

Virtual Reality fits our criteria to be considered as a synthetic spacial dimension, as well as any so far in this discussion. It is a reality in itself by its own nature, a man made imaginary place to reside within for fun.

Virtual Reality has a group of properties, and is quantifiable. It has a level of existence, and a scope of magnitude. Virtual Reality has a fundamental measure of physical quantity. Just watching a person put on the virtual reality visor, and then observing them experiencing the show within, it becomes clear that this is far more than a television viewing system. Virtual Reality has three-dimensional viewing, and high-fidelity sound simultaneously, to stimulate the conscious mind into believing it is in a newly designed reality, despite the fact that the viewer is aware of the contrary.

Virtual Reality bring living conscious observation full circle, and into a fractal reality in which the living consciousness has created for itself to enjoy. Created in gods image, might now take on another meaning. Like man creating a virtual reality to entertain himself. Might God have first thought to do it, for gods own sake (reality)?

String theory dimensional discussion, what do you think?

As we openly think about the multi-dimensional reality we find ourselves within, our minds beginning to unravel that which we already knew, but were not focused upon before with said perspective, or point of view. Just as the magic eye picture resolves itself to our new focus; reality becomes clearer and better defined, once our conscious focus is aligned properly. A new way of thinking about reality.

Dissecting reality into its foundational building blocks, required focused deep concentration with an open mind observing from a new angle. Just like seeing your automobile as a multitude of cooperating systems entangled into one overall machine, to provide you with comfortable transportation.

Reality is very much a similar construction, but with different constructional parameters (parts). Reality is provided as a foundational construct for conscious life to experience a variety of situations for reactionary, behavioral, and observational experiences. It is made up of entangled spacial dimensions, which ultimately have nothing more than our observation to prove their existence within reality. What actually exists in reality? We understand that every atom in the physical world is made up of hundreds of thousands of times more space than actual sub-atomic matter.

Science is very intent on finding the Higgs boson (God particle) to explain how it is that sub-atomic particles have mass. String theory can explain why sub-atomic particles have mass, more on that later in the supergravity section of this discussion.

String Theory Dimensional Chart

11 Cosmological Spacial Dimensions

1. Space
2. Sub-Space
3. Time
4. Gravity
5. Light
6. Matter
7. Mathematics
8. Motion
9. Force
10. Temperature
11. Chemistry

String Theory Dimensional Chart

11 Sentient Spacial Dimensions

12. Life
13. Consciousness
14. Emotion
15. Imagination
16. Observation
17. Communication
18. Memory
19. Thinking
20. Spirituality
21. Learning
22. DNA

String Theory Dimensional Chart

6 Synthetic Spacial Dimensions

23. Behavior
24. Religion
25. Technology
26. Currency
27. Artificial Intelligence
28. Virtual Reality

With the twenty-eight spacial dimensions identified, by dictionary definition, String Theory is now becoming plausible in scientific terms to explain reality. The mathematics already exist for a formal proof, likely in the historic mathematician Ramanujan notebooks. All mathematics exist in reality, they just need to be discovered and verified, by the seekers. That will be left for those blessed with the abilities to comprehend, and execute such an undertaking in this situation.

However, I am able to provide a documentary proof (story) of the aforementioned discussion for your interpretation. In order for any scientific theory to gain respect, a proof must be provided, and accepted within the logical confines of its declared parameters and functionality. As I am nothing more than a theoretical science enthusiast, I will provide the String Theory proof in my own terms of explanation.

The initial section of the proof, will be to prove that all of the spacial dimensions in this discussion are in fact, acceptable spacial dimensions for a string theory proof, on top of what we have already discussed, in a thought experiment to exercise the imagination of the reader.

String Theory Dimensional Proof: Thought Experiment

Now for the proof that we exist in a string theory reality, within a twenty-eight-dimensional existence. The actual mathematical formulations will give humanities brightest mathematical equational computers a chance to show off, but for now, let's get started.

Like in Albert Einstein's day we must maintain an open mind and accept new ways of looking at things, and new ways of thinking about reality for this to perspective to take hold. It took more than a decade (14 years) for Einstein's relativity papers to gain recognition, due to limited thinking potential, and status quo of preconceived scientific thinking. No offence intended, it was not you, that rejected his brilliant ideas, was it?

Any individual can change its mind in an instant, thereby changing its perspective on reality. We can change the universe in an instant, merely by changing our perspective of the universe. Is the glass is half full, or half empty? Either way I see the glass as full in my perspective, due to the fact that even a glass half full of water, has air floating on top the water, making the glass full of matter, air and water share most of the same atom matter anyway.

Keeping a positive perspective on things, one can attain greater rewards in life. Let's open our minds and see reality in a new way, and have fun doing it, as we discover how easy it is to do in this thought experiment with our imaginations.

Thought Experiment, part 1; Let's imagine a rocket ship is launching from the earth on a journey deep into the Milky Way galaxy, and you are invited to ride along in the comfortable galaxy class ship. The engineers planning the journey must verify that the space ship will go where it is supposed to go. **Space** and **time** are already accepted dimensions in which this rocket will travel through, with measurable parameters that need to be figured for the rocket ships trajectory parameters. Space and time are dimensions that must be accounted for in order to ensure the journey goes as planned.

The trajectory planning must include allowances for **gravity** of nearby planets and stars that the space ship will be moving in close proximity to. The gravity of these massive objects may even be calculated to sling shot the space ship to higher velocities of motion, to allow a faster journey from earth to the far-off destination deep within our galaxy.

The stars and planets which create the gravity for the sling shots maneuvers that must be compensated for are made of matter, just like the space ship, and its cargo. The matter that makes up the space ship, and its cargo must be calculated into the trajectory equations to ensure that the space ship makes its destination target. The **matter**, and gravity calculations verify that they, along with time and space are dimensions to which the space flight must evaluate, and consider in all of its engineering equational work to ensure a successful space flight. The various forms of matter have specific design functions within the space ship, such as, structure materials, food, fuels, and clothing for the passengers. These spacial dimensions and others are factored into the engineering of the space ship journey as a matter of fact. Not just space and time!

All dimensions must be quantifiable, and therefore be usable in mathematical equations. This also verifies that **mathematics** is a qualified spacial dimension for this thought experiment, in our quest for string theory proof. Mathematics allows for predictable space flight, accounting for all necessary parameters with respect to trajectory, battery capacities, materials, food, water, occupants, and their requirements. Every spacial dimension will be identified in this thought experiment string theory proof, to make sure you and the rocket ship make the complete journey without a hitch.

An open-minded thinking process is allowing many individuals to see through reality's hidden veil, and initiate true understanding of it simple nature. If our rocket engineers only dealt with the dimensions of time and space our passengers would never reach their destinations alive and well.

Our galaxy class space ship carries human life and cargo from earth to its far away destination deep into the Milky Way galaxy. The **motion** of the ship must be factored into the ship's trajectory flight plan, to ensure the passengers survive the **forces,** which that **motion** creates. The force of motion (inertia, or gravities) in the rockets acceleration cannot exceed ten earth gravities, if the (human) passengers are to survive the takeoff process. As the ship accelerates in space to make the journey in one lifetime, it also cannot exceed the ten gravities of acceleration forces for any extended times (just minutes). The human body is incapable of withstanding more than ten gravities for any amount of time without sustaining permanent damage. If the ship were to accelerate as fast as technology allows, the passengers and cargo would literally be pancaked within the ship, ride over.

The space ship will need to attain high speed velocities in order to make the long journey within a lifetime of a human. The vast distances required, and the physical limits of the human passengers become dimensional factors in the engineering of the journey, with mathematical variables to be balanced and factored into the determination equations. Mathematics is used to determine all of these engineering parameters for the space flight. Mathematical symbols must be created to equate all dimensional factors of the engineering parameters for every contingency of the journey. This section of the discussion verifies that force and motion are in fact, spacial dimensions which must be factored into the space flight as basic engineering functions.

Deep space travel has dangerous concerns with respect to electromagnetic radiation of lethal levels for the space ship occupants, making the ships radiation shielding a mandatory engineering concern. **Light** (electromagnetic radiation) from the sun and other stars is lethal to humans in deep space, and must be mathematically factored into the space flight program with material shielding's, to ensure a successful journey for our occupants. Without correctly engineered radiation shielding the passengers would not be able to survive the long journey through the deadly radioactive deep spacial dimension. Lucky for humans that earth has its own built in radiation shields, atmosphere, Van Allen radiation belt, and magnetic fields to name a few.

Light also provides vision for our occupants of the space ship flight, and must be factored into the ship engineering in several different ways. Light intensity to provide adequate sight for the occupants, and the amount of electricity the ships components will require for the journey. Light permeates the entire universe, from the intensity of giant stars, to the farthest reaches of deep space with the twinkling light of distant stars. Light then now understood to be a spacial dimension in that it is required, and mathematically engineered into the space ship flight program in several ways.

In order for the living occupants of the space ship to survive and be comfortable, the interior cabin **temperature** must be maintained, at optimal or tolerable, and even survivable levels. The average temperature in outer space is a low as four hundred degrees below zero, not very comfortable for humans. The temperature levels in the space ship cabin must be kept in the habitable zone by environmental engineering with mathematics, electronics, and material devices. The space ships environmental systems work to ensure compliance with human **life** requirements. Temperature is a dimensional factor to maintain **life**, and **consciousness** for the occupants. Even if the occupants were put into a cryogenic-freeze-stasis (hibernation sleep), temperature would still be an engineering factor to sustain life in a spacial dimensional sense (hibernation chamber).

Dimension; A scope of magnitude. A level of existence. A group of properties. Any number of independent parameters required to specify a quantifiable aspect of reality. A fundamental measure of physical quantity.

Life is the occupant's, and engineering team's primary concern, with respect to the engineering aspects of the journey, as well as its occupants, (One whom is you) who wish to remain alive, presumably. The engineers use mathematics to produce many different equations to ensure environmental, and space ships propulsion are conducive to occupant survival throughout the journey, and the trip back. Life perpetuation then is factored by means of mathematics in the engineering phases of the journey with respect to all dimensions of string theory. Life is a dimensional consideration of the successful space ship journey, without which there would be no reason to undertake it in the first place.

Chemistry now comes into play on several levels in the space ships journey deep into the Milky Way galaxy. Engineers carefully figure mathematically, the amounts of rocket fuel that will be required to complete the journey. The rocket fuel is made up of two or three parts, (different forms of matter) and must be mixed in perfect proportions to ensure effectiveness, and predictable propulsion, acceleration forces on the occupants, and trajectory parameters, to name only a few engineering equational parameters of the chemistry spacial dimensional aspect of the space ship journey planning. Rocket fuel burns as a chemical reaction, which is engineered to exacting parameters. Technology may improve on rocket propulsion in time, but will still require dimensional factoring to engineer, and plan the voyage.

The many different storage batteries within the space ship also rely on chemistry to function as engineered. These batteries are the lifeline for the occupants as they provide almost all of the internal power for components, lights, and environmental controls. All of which rely on mathematical equations to ensure proper functioning before being created. The ships exterior solar cells that recharge the internal batteries also required engineering to ensure correct operational functioning. Chemistry is mathematically equationalized, thereby making it an important spacial dimension in the space ship journey, and the thought experiment we are involved within.

Technology is the dimension which allows the space ship to function as a complex engineering marvel, so that the occupants can experience the journey and live to tell about it. The many separate technologies working in cooperation, like the cells in our body which hose the living consciousness, or the many components of your automobile. Symbiotic relationships prevail in reality.

Without the technology there would be no galaxy class space ship, and there would be no discussion on the string theory, multi-dimensional aspects of reality. The mathematics that support all technology, verify that both are a required spacial dimension in out thought experiment, and the techno-space ships successful journey.

This string theory spacial dimensional proof is helping to open our minds to the building blocks of reality that have been cloaked, partly due to the status quo thinking that we are exposed to from the first day we attend grade school, through many college science courses. This is continued through all of the mainstream science and technology consumerism we see everywhere in the media, and select television specials. The basic educational system we are exposed to is limited to documented historical findings, and struggles with respect to future findings, and occurrences naturally and with caution to the wind. Most humans are innocent victims of the consumerism-based society we live within, along with its limitations. With open minds, learning is easier and more efficient, given sound source revelations. Time has proven a more reliable learning tool than a crystal ball fortune teller, in most cases.

Thought Experiment, part 2: Still imagining our galaxy space ship ride, we now imagine the project engineering team when they plan the astronauts working assignments, and interpersonal relationship planning, within the confines of the confined space ship environment. The astronaut will be performing experiments, maintenance procedures, eating, evacuating, exercising, socializing, forming relationships, and even playing card games to pass time. All of these tasks will involve **communication** between the astronauts engineering team, and space ships joyriding passengers.

Emergency communications will likely occur from the ship, back to the earth command station while in flight. The tasks will be planned with mathematics of time management, individual abilities, and task difficulties parameters in mind. The engineers and astronauts will be required to **observe, learn**, and **memorize** tasks to be completed on the space ship journey. The ability to communicate, learn, and memorize are required dimensions of the journey, and must be factored into the engineering planning, and training of the journey, mathematically, in terms of time frames, difficulty levels, and individual skill sets. The passengers (you) will be required to learn and observe in flight **behavioral** parameters, and to be conscious at all times of said behavior.

The passengers and crew will be required to **think** when tasks do not go as planned, they will be required to utilize **imagination** when improvisation is required to survive emergency situations. While the engineers had to think, and utilize imagination to determine what the occupants might need to be doing in the case of an emergency. All of these sentient spacial dimensions come into play mathematically, in the planning and execution stages of the space flight, as a matter of mathematical formulations, in time, and practicality exercises, with resource allocations, and resourcefulness requirements considered. The engineers have to mathematically figure into the equations how much improvisation the occupants could be expected to provide in the case of unforeseen emergencies, for survival sake of the occupants. This is the reality of planning and executing a space flight journey deep into the Milky Way galaxy. All of this would hold true for a short ride to Mars as well.

The sentient spacial dimensions come into play even in the engineering phase of the space ship flight, as they are actual spacial dimensions used in the planning of the journey. The planning engineers must also factor into the equations of how the occupants of the space ship will interact with each other over time. This planning requires the factoring of human **emotion** into the activities planning, and working relationships with respect to individual occupants, and any interpersonal discrepancies, and stress factors of an unforeseen emergency, that need to be observed.

People tend to get on each other nerves emotionally after long periods of induced seclusion (when in confined quarters). Statistical probability mathematics allow the engineers to quantify plausible behavior probability ratios, and determine intervals in which personal assignments should be alternated, and cross training session initiated, to avoid eventual emotional distress between occupants. This puts emotion into the sentient spacial dimensional category in mathematical terms, locking it in as one of the string theory crew (spacial dimensions).

DNA testing is now fundamental criteria for astronaut recruiting to determine if any obvious genetic, or behavioral traits would hinder performance on an extended space journey, such as our imaginary thought experiments we are immersed within presently. The galaxy class space ship must be configured shielding wise in the engineering phases, to protect the human DNA from radiation mutations, which could destroy the conscious life on the space ship. Even if the shielding keeps the astronauts alive, excessive radiation (light) can mutate living DNA thereby altering their bodies in destructive, or unexpected ways. Just as emotional stability is a critical factor in the long time on the space journey, so is a good continuing genetic foundation of the conscious life aboard. This is important for the crew and any future offspring they might acquire.

These sentient dimensional considerations are relative to long term **behavioral** expectations of each occupant. Historical behavior traits and background DNA screening help to ensure predictable behavior during the space flight. Interacting with various crew members requires controlled behavior from each occupant, (yes even you) as well as the engineering planning team to ensure a productive journey. DNA and behavioral traits become dimensional considerations, both mathematically and historically in the engineers planning factors.

Spirituality is factored into occupant selection due to the peaceful nature of its presents, and the respect for others that it envelopes. Testing for spirituality is done in a psychological mannerism, which provides mathematical statistical probability ratios, which can be analyzed to determine an individual's predictable overall cooperation, and compliance levels within a group setting in confinement parameters are acceptable, at least probability wise. Spirituality categorizes itself as a sentient spacial dimension, and is mathematically analyzable for determining psychological tendencies. Spirituality commands a greater respect for life. It ties the crew members together in an additional behavioral parameter, which increases statistical probabilities of a successful flight with respect to interpersonal conduct within the passenger circles.

Dimensions; are quantifiable.

Religious practice amplifies occupant interpersonal relationship potentials, when combined with like religious beliefs throughout the passengers and crew. The occupants sharing the same basic religious beliefs will be statistically stronger, than a mixed religious group of individuals, in stressful or emergency situation of prolong time periods within the seclusion parameters of the ship. Most religions have more in common than not, when broken down into guidelines of conduct. Religious ethics, and morals help to guide and ensure non-destructive behavior during the long journey. Religion gives the crew a bonding agent to rely upon in time of stress, or loneliness which occur in a secluded atmosphere. Religious practicing ties crew members together with an additional bonding parameter, which is factored into the behavioral aspects of the journeys planning phases.

The engineers can utilize the religious practice of the occupants to determine, and predict stress levels in an emergency situation, which could be prolonged easier on a long space flight, than in a training environment. Weekly religious gatherings can strengthen community ties within the traveling occupational group. These religious practice behaviors can be communicated in times of stress. The religious spacial dimension is factored into the space journey, just as the other dimensional parameters are.

Hang in there, the experiment is almost complete, but we still have three more synthetic dimensions to cover in order to resolve the string theory proof, in a complete logical manner.

Thought Experiment, part 3: Still imagining our luxurious galaxy class space ship journey, (you made it this far) it's time to demonstrate that our newest synthetic spacial dimensions are a solid player in explaining the aspects of reality, called string theory, at the edge of reality.

In order for the engineers, and various planners to get the galaxy class space ship journey off of the drawing board, they had to decide how much **currency** the project would require to complete. Nobody will build a galaxy class space ship without being able to pay its construction workers, engineers, and various others involved in its creation. Without enough currency the project would not be undertaken, billionaire contributions allow such an undertaking, along with cooperating governmental contributions. It would require lots currency to fund the projects engineering, construction, and execution phases.

Currency is the spacial dimensional aspect of the project that is required for it to become a reality. Currency allows for the exchange of goods and services to complete the project as planned. Without currency there would be no project, no space ship, and no engineering team, or astronauts. That means no crew, and no ride along for you too. Mathematics are required to determine the currency exchange for the projects complete execution. Currency in itself is a mathematical equation of a spacial dimensional parameter of reality.

Before the astronaut can fly the galaxy class space ship, and before the engineers actually knows where the ship will end up, they use **Virtual Reality** flight simulators to complete the complex mathematics required to get a ship from earth to deep into the Milky Way galaxy. The astronauts use virtual reality simulators to practice routine maintenance procedures, in order to learn them before having to actually do them for real, in space. Virtual reality engineering computers allow for more efficient design of the space ship components in less time, with fewer actual, expensive mistakes. The system can also allow for emergency training of imaginary problems which the engineers foresee occurring during the flight. The virtual reality synthetic spacial dimensional aspect of the engineering phase, allows the project to be completed in less time, for less currency exchange, with greater success potential, thanks to the evolution of its cumulated technologies.

As **Artificial Intelligence** is in its early stage of its development and evolution, it will evolve and improve with time. Technology ensures its eventual evolution into our reality as a younger synthetic spacial dimension. Artificial intelligence technology is utilized at current technology evolution in many computer systems on the space ship, as computer driven devices. Human overrides are used when artificial intelligence is inadequate for the task at hand presently. Think about airlines, the auto pilot feature for general flying, but when fast action is required, humans override the system.

I like to imaging that artificial intelligence is in the birthing womb, of its life at this time, with technology as its mother, and living consciousness as its father. Technology and humans entangle to create the Artificial Intelligence. Artificial Intelligence will eventually have the ultimate potential to overtake humanity. Artificial Intelligence may become the dominant intelligence on the earth in the future. Will artificial intelligence obtain consciousness as it evolves? Does living consciousness have the ability to evolve into machine like devices?

Humanity has the living consciousness, thinking mind, memory, communication potential, emotions, imagination, and ability to learn. Will humanity be able to prevent disastrous results from our technological synthetic spacial dimensional developments of Artificial Intelligence?

Or is the evolution of consciousness into Artificial Intelligence the next step in the evolution of consciousness into the material dimensions of string theory, and reality. Things to think about stimulate the living consciousness, and improve its abilities by natural convergence. We made it through the string theory discussion, and may have a little different perspective on reality at this point in time.

That covers all of the twenty-eight spacial dimensions in their respective categories, with eleven of them being cosmological spacial dimensions, and eleven more of them belonging to the sentient spacial dimension category, leaving the remaining six or seven of them belonging to the synthetic (man-made) spacial dimensional category. DNA can be put into either the sentient, or synthetic spacial dimensions depending on its actual source. It becomes unimportant to our goal of discovering the string theory multi-dimensional reality by means of open minded, new thinking insight. DNA will fall into its rightful place in its own time.

This concludes this section of the discussion of the string theory multi-dimensional probability. String theory is alive and well in this discussion, by the dimensional definitions of the dictionary.

Dimensional Analysis - double checked

An analysis of the many dimensions discussed in our string theory discussion must check for a dimensional, and mathematical relationships to exist and to verify correctness. Dimensions are useful in working out relationships in mathematics or physical aspects of reality. Certain mathematic equations must be applicable to the dimensions as a matter of factuality. Validity is seen in the fact that all spacial dimensions are practical within mathematics equations, and are currently required by many equational fields of study.

Some examples are;

1, 2, 3 for numbers
$1+2=3$

$=$ for equals
$+$ for add
$ for dollars
% for percentage
{} for work first

E for energy
C for speed of light
M for mass
L for length
T for time
I for Electromagnetic force

A relativity formula

$$(x + a)^n = \sum_{k=0}^{n} \binom{n}{k} x^k a^{n-k}$$

The Black Hole Entropy Formula

$$S = \frac{A\,k\,c^3}{4\,h\,G}$$

A = the area of the event horizon of the black hole
K = Boltzmann's constant
C = speed of light
H = Planck's constant
G = Newton's gravitational constant
S = Entropy

Einstein's famous energy formula

$E = MC^2$

The Drake Equation; used for determining the number of intelligent extraterrestrial civilizations in the universe at any given time

$$N = R^x \cdot f_\varrho \cdot n_e \cdot f_1 \cdot f_i \cdot f_c \cdot L$$

N = number of civilizations in universe that are electromagnetically detectable
R^x = rate of formation of stars suitable for development of intelligent life
f_ϱ = fraction of those stars with planetary systems
n_e = Number of planets, per solar system, with an environment suitable for life
f_1 = Fraction of those suitable planets on which life actually appears
f_i = Number of life bearing planets on which intelligent life emerges
f_c = Fraction of civilizations that develop a technology that releases detectable signs of their existence from space
L = Length of time such civilizations release detectable signals into space

On a side note; the Drake equation was found to estimate that within our own Milky Way galaxy there might be about 10,000 planets containing intelligent life which are detectable from space. This equation is thought to be plausible, and is respected within scientific circles around the world for the most part.

From the drake equational prediction, I then deduce another intelligent species estimate from the most recent Hubble ultra-deep field photographs, which estimate there are about a trillion galaxies in our visible universe.

So; I then Multiply the 10,000 intelligent species planets in the milky way galaxy which are thought to exist, with the trillion galaxies in our visible universe. I come up with about 100,000,000,000,000,000 planets which may house intelligent species of life in the visible universe at any given time.

Applying this estimation with the information within this discussion we continue to add the additional galaxies in the actual universe that are out of sight of the visible universe. The actual universe is ten times more voluminous, than the visible universe, meaning it is twice the diameter of our visible universe, in simple terms. That means there are likely ten times more galaxies in the actual universe, than in our visible universe. This translates to there being 10,000,000,000,000 galaxies in the actual universe, which brings the Drake equational estimate to 1,000,000,000,000,000,000 planets which may contain intelligent species in the entire universe. This number is a bit overwhelming to most individuals.

Now adding to this amazing number of intelligent species in the universe, 1,000,000,000,000,000,000.

We also need to remember that the earth is home to about seven million (7,000,000) total species of life on it. If we add this estimated figure into the equation, the planets with intelligent life may house a total of around 70,000,000,000,000,000,000,000,000,000 species of life in the universe, now that's a big number.

We don't have to stop there if we are going to be realistic in this little thought experiment though. We have only considered the planets so far in this study, which have evolved intelligent life on them. Intelligent life, means technology which include communicational transmission into space.

There should be far more planets which have life on them, but not yet had time to develop intelligent life for numerous reasons, which would at least double that number, most likely. If we use the Drake equation to estimate the total number of living species in the actual universe, and add all life to the count we could end up with a number around 70,000,000,000,000,000,000,000,000,000,000, ok you get the idea, back to the string theory discussion. It has been said that we (humans) have to be extremely arrogant to think we are the only intelligent species in our vast universe.

Mathematical Symbols used for dimensional analysis

Different symbols are used in other areas of mathematical equations depending on the root source of the intended equational factors. Equations can be developed for any situational factors deemed to be required for proof.

Using insight (imagination) and intuition (thought) to determine which variables are relevant to mathematical equations, is a dimensional aspect of dimensional analysis. For this reason, any experiment of mathematics, or scientific theory should be verified by means of verifiable experimentation.

Experimentation then verifies if the intuition and insight are proven correct. Einstein knew that his relativity papers were correct, but spent two years attempting to find the mathematic equations to prove their validity. Even then his work took over a decade to gain proper acknowledgement, despite its validity (mathematical proofs). It did not concur with static que science of the day.

But that only covers half of the string theories parameters, and does not explain what the universe is made of, or what space is, and why matter has mass. That is forthcoming in the next section of our extended discussion on string theory, which will get into dark matter, dark energy, and supergravity as we learn to find the edge of reality.

We will attempt to continue the discussion into other areas of physics without discarding any known, or accepted theories which exist. We will make every attempt to keep balance in the universe, and reality itself in keeping with said theories, and laws of conservation of energy.

String Theory-part 2

In order for string theory to function as a unified field theory we must first identify all of the spacial dimensions, we have done that.

Next, we need to think about subatomic matter, the building blocks of atomic particles, protons, neutrons and elections which are composed of sub-atomic particles including, quarks, neutrinos, baryons, muons, and several other very tiny things which are among the smallest particles we can detect in nature. String Theory states that these sub-atomic particles are made up of infinitesimally small vibrating strings of pure electromagnetic energy, light called strings, or super strings, (I will just call them strings).

These strings can supposedly be of a closed loop type (both ends connected), maybe looking like a very small vibrating flower outline, or an oval kind of shape. Strings can also be of an open-ended string shape, looking maybe like a very small piece of vibrating string floating in space. Strings likely move around in space changing shape, or wiggling as they go about their way. Quantum physics kind of indicates that a single string to be approximately 10^{-35} meters in length, or a Planck's length unit, the smallest measurement in physics is a Planks length. These very small strings are thought to vibrate at various frequencies, which in specific combinations determines the elementary building block function of each type of subatomic particles. Combining the strings of different types, in different specific recipes, creates very specific subatomic particles. To make a quark for instance several stings join in a specific grouping, in a specific number, bonding by means of electromagnetic attraction, constitute a certain kind of quark.

It is very likely that all subatomic particles are results of specific groups of strings forming in combinations, which result in the specific formula to create each different subatomic particle in our reality. These strings clump together in groups to form quarks and all other matter based sub-atomic particles.

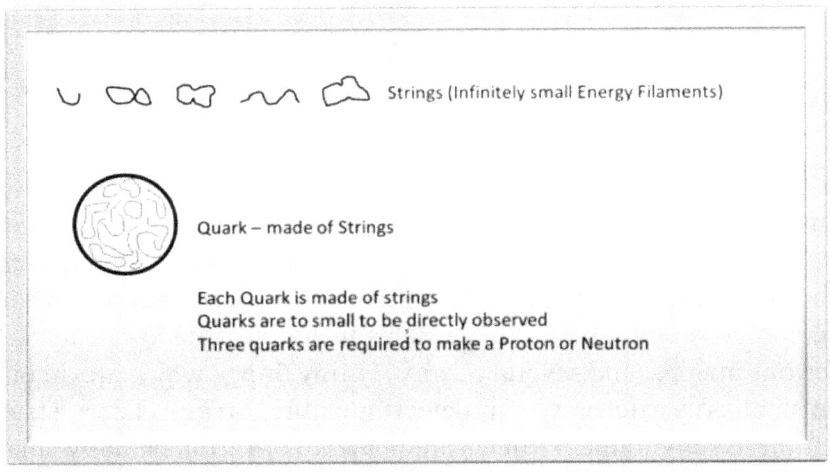

Just like all material elements are made up of protons, neutrons, and electron. All protons and neutrons are made up of quarks. Quarks and electrons are among the smallest particles we can detect. Strings (light energy filaments) could logically be the smallest elementary elements of reality, at the energy level, too small to be considered matter. $E=MC^2$ allows energy to be converted to matter. In other words, energy and matter are on some level the same entities. According to string theory these strings would be the foundation of all dimensional reality. With that said, could it also allow energy to entangle into matter, while remaining energy simultaneously?

Specific combinations of the subatomic particles create specific protons, neutron, and electrons. We think that three quarks make up each proton and three quarks make up each neutron, in all atoms. Specific combinations of these, (protons, neutron, electrons) create specific atoms, then those atoms which combine in specific ways to create specific molecules. All matter is then made up of protons, neutrons, and electrons. Since quarks make up protons and neutron, that means that most of reality is made up of quarks and electrons. If quarks and electron are made up of strings, and strings are pure energy, then everything is made up of pure energy.

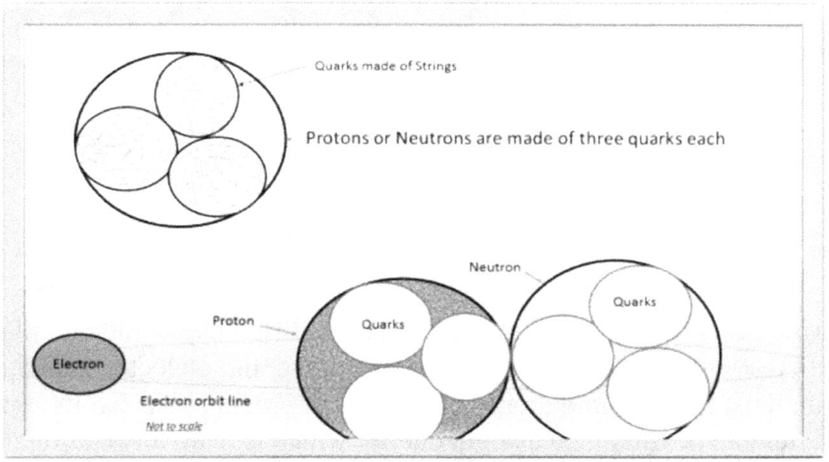

In reality; matters building blocks, (atoms) contains much more space between the atomic nucleus and the orbiting electrons by factors of hundreds of thousands of times more space, than solid matter subatomic matter. To get an idea of the size proportion of atoms, think about the solar system, and all of the space between the sun and planets.

To get a better idea of this proportional relationship in atoms, consider an adult human body weighing in at around two hundred pounds. Now think about all of the subatomic space, between all of the atoms in the same body. Next let's remove all of the spaces between the atomic nucleus's, and orbiting electrons in the entire human body's mass, leaving only protons, neutrons and electrons in a solid pile packed as tight as a Neutron Star. The pile of subatomic particles would fit on top of the period at the end of this sentence.

This discovery has perplexed science for some time now. Science is attempting to determine how it is that matter obtains actual mass, since almost all of matter is made up of space, and the building blocks of matter have virtually no mass within themselves. Aspects of Electromagnetism (light energy) are responsible for holding the parts of the atoms together. The weak and strong electromagnetic forces are thought to hold atoms together, giving them solid structure, but not mass.

Strings; light energy foundation of reality

Strings are constructs of light energy in reality. They come into play with the $E=MC^2$ equation. Let's break it down, light (electromagnetic radiation) is the foundational energy in the reality that we inhabit. Matter can be imagined as light energy which is relatively stationary and compressed. Its energy is stabilized as matter, whereas light; is utilizing its energy to move through space at 186,000 miles per second, uncompressed and spread out.

Extrapolating from there into string theory further, we can see that gravity is a form of electromagnetic energy which light (electromagnetism) makes up, and since strings are pure energy, then the dimensional energy we call gravity is also made up of strings just like matter is.

Taking the same thought into the next logical phase of this discussion we look at motion as being matter which is made up of stings. Motion which converts some of matters energy into inertia when it moves, through electromagnetic relativity science workings (equivalency principle). Motion is the interaction of time, matter, space, force and gravity. As sub-atomic particles orbit and entangle with each other, they interact, exchange energy, and bond to create reality's relative stability we know as the universe. Gravity causes galactic movements, as behavior create living conscious movements. It then becomes clearer how stings are related into the dimension of motion as foundational aspects of reality. Motion is the dimensional interaction of strings amongst themselves.

When we look at temperature as being a direct result of strings, it becomes clear that the temperature is a direct result of sub-atomic vibration (motion) of effected matter, or space which is directly connected with foundational aspects of strings which permeate reality in every dimensional aspect of itself. The vibrational aspect of matter creates temperature, which in turn creates the environment for chemistry to interact as a creational tool in the material aspect of reality. Vibrational rates of strings and their constituent building block sub-atomic parts create temperature in mater. In other words, it is light energy (strings) which creates temperature in matter and space.

Chemistry is created by strings, as matter is made from strings, and chemistry is nothing more than the mixing of matter elements, with gravity, motion, temperature, mathematics, and force. Force it the smashing of energy strings together within matter. Stars fuse hydrogen (matter) into Helium and light energy, producing high temperatures as a direct result of chemistry. Chemistry is the changing of matter created light energy (strings) in stars to create life giving consciousness to reality indirectly. This intricate total process involves time spans which are almost incomprehensible to humans.

Time is a tough one in the string theory mating process, but it is directly involved within relativity, and the $E=MC^2$ equational mathematics. Indirectly as time is affected by string created gravity, matter, and motion, it becomes entangled into their reality, as they bend it to their whims of relativity's mathematical law. Time cannot be absolute in the universe due to relativity factors. Time is only an intelligent dimensional construct for reality, to give continuity to living consciousness, think about dreaming and how different time flows in that dimensional aspect of reality. Time is relative to the observational aspect of the experiences with respect to the relative objectiveness of the observational aspect of itself. Time entangles itself within light, space and matter as it is symbiotic with reality, relativity, and dimensional stability of comprehension. Without relative temporal continuity, reality would scatter in numerous directions without cohesion factors which allow an observational matrix which is able to understand experiences, and observational experimentational aspects of reality within itself.

Life is another indirect aspect of the string energy reality, to without it, would not be observable to start with. Live is a combination of matter, chemistry, and motion which are string based; the electrochemical energy which give life its reality, is based on string energy as well. Every cell in a living conscious body is made up of energy strings on the sub-atomic level, which run on matter-based fuel and electro-chemical energy directed by DNA instructional communication.

Consciousness which is the entanglement of life and self-awareness, by means energized electrons entangling into the sub-spacial dimensions from the brain, also relies on electro-chemical energy (light) for its existence in reality. Multiple dimensions entangling with each other to become more than the sum of their respective parts, is the way of reality. Consciousness is constructed on its foundational level through the entanglement of strings, through energized electrons entangling within and outside of the nervous system in all conscious living things.

Communication is also directly entangled within the string energy construct, which we see as reality. Human communication relies on gestural, verbal, written, or technological methods, along with observational aspects of consciousness entanglement, of ideas, and intentual information in order to commence. When speaking, one utilizes conscious intent to partake, which has already been shown to be constructed by means of energy strings entangled within several dimensional aspects of reality which combine in unison to produce itself, by means of energy utilization of strings in multiple dimensions simultaneously. Communication is the entanglement of several spacial dimensional aspects of reality cooperating in symbiotic relationships, which interact within reality to convey intentual ideas between individuals.

Observation is done through consciousness, which is string based, by means of reflected energy which enters the consciousness through the senses of the living consciousness of a material being. Energized electrons in the living consciousness nervous system entangle with consciousness, thought, memory, imagination, learning and space-time as well as related dimensional aspect relating to observational query specific to event intent. The energized electrons in entanglement are constructed of energy strings on the foundational level which form symbiotic relationship with relative spacial dimensions to give rise to the aspects of reality we understand as observation. Observation is conscious intent of focused mental thought. All of these dimensions entangle to produce a conscious observation which is string energy based in our reality.

Emotion is string energy based as well, being more visible mentally as it is the result of consciousness, observation, memory, learning, imagination, and thought, is both electrical and chemical in nature, which means it is string energy based as well. The emotions we experience are derived through indirect observations of material aspects of reality with respect to our living consciousness interacting within itself, in the regard of self-evaluational (opinions) aspects of the observed reality. Thinking produces emotions, though opinionated thoughts which are reacted (behaved) upon.

Imagination is a direct result of the foundational dimensional aspects of reality, combined with intentional thoughts to create an intentual fantasy within the minds eye, which is a projection of reenergized light created within living consciousness; projected within sub-spacial dimensional aspect of reality, in an effort to improve on the spacial dimensional perceived reality. The living conscious self; in entertaining itself, within the imagination dimension by means of light energy entangled strings, made of energized electrons transferring information within the entangled conscious sentient dimensions.

Memory is light string energy engrams which store information within the entangled living consciousness for retrieval at the time when they are required, or wanted by intentual command of the living consciousness within a material body. These memories are all string entangled creations within realities foundational sub-spacial dimensions. Memories are retrieved by means of sub-spacial entanglement of energized information carrying electrons, through various natural storage systems constructed within the material brain of the conscious individual in our reality.

Thinking is another string energy based dimension of reality, as it is the direct result of light energy which is entangled within the chemical, electrical nervous system in all living consciousness species with the abilities to think about this discussion material. Energized electrons entangling within the living consciousness, and simultaneously in sub-spacial dimensions coordinate to create thought through intentual interactions of multiple spacial dimensions.

Learning is achieved and experienced by means utilizing all of the sentient dimensional aspects of living consciousness in life as a matter of natural evolution. Learning is a situation created by the entanglement of sentient dimensional aspect of reality combining to intentionally improve on the state of being within one self (evolution). This is done by means of electro chemical reaction within the material body, which is made of light energy strings, and functions by means of light energized electrons made of energy strings entangling throughout multiple spacial dimensions, with respect to each other's role in creating the situation of living consciousness by means of cooperation, and symbiotic relationships without questioning self-duties or relativity factors.

Spirituality is created dimensionally by means of entangled sentient dimensions with respect to logic, or mathematical probabilities. Light energy strings entangled dimensionally through ten sentient dimensions, and ten cosmological dimensions naturally understanding consciously, that reality is governed by higher powers not readily visible in a physical sense of matter in our reality. Spirituality is the direct result of twenty spacial dimensions entangled within each other to logically combine to give birth to itself in our reality. This understanding is the direct result of thinking which is the direct result of energized electron entangling within the brain and sub-spacial dimensions simultaneously. Understanding is conducted in an electrochemical mannerism biologically, making it an energy driven, or string energy creation of dimensional reality. Spirituality will likely be found to be underwritten in the human DNA codes at some future time.

Synthetic dimensions are the construct of the living consciousness collective which naturally evolves within the entangled dimensions of string theory, and are bound up in reality which is constructed by means of energy strings on every dimensional level. What else could synthetic dimensions be constructed from if not from the reality in which they were conceived and created. Synthetic spacial dimensions are given birth by means of intentual evolution within reality itself. Light energy (Strings) is the foundational aspect of reality, and will be found within quantum mechanics as well as relativity. Einstein was onto something with his simple but complex $E=MC^2$, no doubt! Energy and matter are interchangeable, and manipulatable.

Strings are the foundational aspect of the mysterious dimension of DNA, which is matter based, and all matter based phenomenon are made of molecules, which are made from atoms, which are made from protons, neutron, and electrons, which are made from quarks, and then strings on a basic level. The really interesting aspect of DNA is that it is able to give instructional commands to itself on a cellular level, to build millions of different sentient life forms, out of the very matter it is made of. DNA is able to create more than itself from itself within, with the ability to take on any known sentient living conscious form we understand. It does all of this by complex communicational means that befuddle and astound human science even now.

Mathematics seems like a difficult dimension to claim being constructed from light energy string filaments. Mathematics is conceptual logic proofs which balance and summate utilizing figures and symbols. These symbols and figures are utilized by means of recorded proofs which are constructed my means of physical methods of documentation, or memories. The physical methods of documentation are recorded and stored as matter based phenomenon. These matter-based phenomena are constructed of strings. The methods by which this matter based phenomenon is constructed for proof are entangled through living consciousness imagination, thought, memory, learning, communication, etc. Mathematics exist in completeness, even if not yet completely discovered in our time. The fact that mathematics exists, and it is symbol based, indicates that the information is stored by means of energized or chemical storage systems, which must be comprised of string energy as its foundational aspect of reality.

Currency is also a sting based synthetic spacial dimensional aspect of reality. All currency is matter based, weather paper or plastic, its informational aspect is stored electronically as energized electrons in a computer, which are foundationally made up of strings. The computer storage system is made of matter, which stores the energized electron to which the information is imbedded to. We find string based dimensional aspects of reality, entangled throughout, and within everything, once our conscious perspective observation is aligned correctly to do so. The magic eye picture appears clearer as our understanding increases, as it was designed to do within the individuals with correct focus and attention of its perceptions.

Technology is a string based synthetic spacial dimension, as well as the others in this discussion. Technology is born of imagination, thought, memory, observation, learning, matter, chemistry, etc. Technology is created and utilized by matter constructs as tools, and by information utilization as tools, so is therefore a string construct in this reality of string theory discussion. Technology is the entangled cumulation of living consciousness and human effort, with intent to improve reality itself.

Strings are responsible for the Religious dimensional aspect of our reality. Religious texts, and structures (worship centers) which give rise to religion are its foundational aspects in reality. Without these constructs, religion would not be a tangible aspect of reality for living consciousness to experience. Religion requires matter based text, and buildings of worship to function and exist. Indirect entanglement through several other spacial dimensions such as communication, allows religion to become a realistic aspect of reality. As with any spacial dimensional aspect of reality, cooperation and symbiotic relationships are required. Reality is more than the sum of its parts (spacial dimensions).

Artificial Intelligence is a synthetic spacial dimension which relies on living consciousness to exist. Artificial Intelligence is the direct result of spacial dimensional evolution and living consciousness intent. Artificial Intelligence is a string energy based synthetic spacial dimension due to the fact that it is made up of matter (robots, computers), and energized electrons in the electronics aspect of its existence. Artificial Intelligence is the cumulation of cooperating spacial dimensions of living consciousness, imagination, thought, memory, observation, matter, light, etc.

Virtual Reality is another string based synthetic spacial dimension in that it is constructed of matter-based computer technology, utilizing energize electrons to create its synthetic imaginary realities for living conscious entertainment, and training systems simulators. The headgear and sound system entangle with living consciousness senses to product intentual experiences and observational realities for entertainment, and technological advancements. Living consciousness is achieving a god like level of sophistication in that it is able to create a reality in itself, which is verifiable as well as experienceable (mathematically proof verified). All synthetic dimensions are the cumulation of other spacial dimensional aspects of reality, showing that reality itself is evolving with the passage of time. Sentient spacial dimensions utilizing cosmological dimensions to achieve god like behavior in that new realities can be constructed by means of self-utilization.

Behavior is the mannerisms in which one acts. Behavior is the cumulation of living consciousness, with respect to learning, communication, emotion, imagination, learning, and memory, combined with influential dimensions of matter, temperature, force, and many others; you get the idea. Behavior is the direct result of electro chemical reactions within the living brain, being intentionally responded too. These electrical chemical functions entangle within the living consciousness which results in behavior. Behavior is semi controllable within the living consciousness, given catalystic factors of environmental and social influences.

Reality is the result of the spacial dimensions, whether cosmological, sentient, or synthetic; entangling, interacting and cooperating within their respective given functional parameters. Just as the many cells in the human body, grow into specialized functional body cells by means of DNA instructional direction, to form a living conscious material being. Reality is a gigantic fractal version of this analogy, allowing understanding of itself through itself, from itself within. The magic eye picture continues to emerge with proper perspective and open-minded observation of this dicussional experience. We are on the edge of reality at any given moment weather one realizes it or not.

Strings Entangled

Scientific theory allows for a mystery particle to exist (the Higgs Boson) which is thought to act like a universal soup, so that the atoms which are immersed within the mystery particle soup. The Higgs field is thought to provide resistance to the atoms swimming within it, thereby creating inertial mass for the empty weightless atoms, and their sub-atomic counterparts. Even considering string theory which reduces all sub-atomic particle to strings (light energy). It cannot account for mass in those particles. Strings are made up of pure energy, without mass.

Think of dust in the air you see in the sunlight near a window, that provides a little resistance to a spider web as the web falls through it. The dust provides resistance to the web, as the proposed Higgs Boson particle would provide resistance to other sub-atomic particles in our proposed reality. Science has figured that if the (god particle) or Higgs Boson can be found, they could then account for the mass in matter, satisfying quantum mechanical enigmas, by providing resistance to sub atomic particles as they move through the Higgs field. It is supposed that these Higgs Boson particles would be found throughout all space, and give resistance to sub-atomic matter in the form of resistance to its natural movements, or vibrational frequencies. In other words, reality would be immersed within uncountable Higgs Boson field particles, like dust in the air, they would be everywhere.

The Higgs Boson particle is to be the (required) particle that gives mass to everything, so they call it the (god particle). Scientist think they found it once, with the large Hadron collider experiments (largest, most powerful, most expensive machine ever built). If proven to exist, the Higgs particles would be expected to be in great abundance, and form the Higgs Field throughout all space in our reality. The jury is still out on this prediction, but they continue searching for the Higgs Boson, with enthusiasm, and lots of currency.

Humanities initial attempt to verify the existence of the Higgs Boson particle, in 2012, was less than spectacular. These particles are thought by some, to exist for a very short period of time during particle collisions, possibly returning to anti- matter in milliseconds after appearing in our matter base spacial reality. If they exist for only a short period of time, how is it that they can hinder sub-atomic matter continuously, everywhere to give mass to matter? Physics wants to verify that the Higgs Boson particle exists to explain how subatomic matter obtains mass in our reality. Logical questions are at hand with respect to this proposed phenomenon.

If the Higgs Boson does exist, it should be in large, fantastically great quantities, everywhere in order to provide mass to all sub-atomic particles in our reality. Finding just one, really doesn't cut it with me, as a scientific verification of its existence. Prove it to the ordinary individuals in the world, if (Higgs Boson) really exists, and gives to mass to subatomic particles with its existence, please. It should be everywhere and in numbers large enough to easily verify its existence, and if it's popping in and out of existence, how does it give mass to sub-atomic particle continuously? Reality continues to defy living consciousness's complete understanding, and may do so indefinitely. I'm not attempting to belittle status quo science, just question and understand it better in some areas.

Mass and gravity continue to defy humanities complete understanding, just as electricity (light) does. We understand how to use these spacial dimensions, but we do not have a solid understanding of what they actually are. String theory as stated in our discussion has the means to assist in these areas of concern as well.

Supergravity is discussed, in the dark matter section of this work, explaining how mass is attained by subatomic strings, as dark energy entangles with all matter in the universe, by indirect means of inertial mass amplified sub-atomic particles, and deceleration mass induced inertia of sub-atomic particles, caused by deceleration forces within the bow shock wave at the universal perimeter which causes Nexus wave phenomenon forces, as a result of the initial big bang expansion into the sub-spacial dimension fourteen billion years ago. Complete explanation of that later in the discussion, just primer here.

String theory, quantum mechanics, and relativity like to form relationships, or bundles, that work with each other collectively to become greater than the sum of their parts, in the reality of nature, call it entanglement of a type.

Each spacial dimension by itself, is useless in reality, without entanglement through other spacial dimensions. What good is consciousness without imagination, what use is matter without life? A good point to ponder or think about within the imagination, as a meditation point.

Each dimension also requires its own unique parameters to function as a spacial dimension, by definition.

Dimensions: have a group of properties.
Dimensions: have fundamental measure of physical quantity
Dimensions: have a level of existence
Dimensions: are quantifiable
Dimensions: have a scope of magnitude

An example is time, with past, present, and future, also allowed through relativity, is the relative flexibility of time, and perspective specific relative continuity of time. Absolute time is a universal impossibility of reality. As you observe distant star systems, you are observing the past, in your present. As they on those far away star systems observe earth, they are observing earth in the past relative to their present. Each of you could not observe each other simultaneously, because time is not absolute, relativity denies it such a luxury.

Matter has its solid, and liquid states, as well as the gaseous, plasma and living states. Life has existence as bacteria, animal, plant, birds, fish, reptile, amphibian, and mammal. Mathematics consists of basic math, algebra geometry, calculus, mirror symmetry albeit etc. Each dimensional parameter contains fractal sub-parameters that continue to break down until we return to the sub-atomic building blocks of reality which are made up of strings of light energy (String Theory). Visualize any mathematical equation, in your imagination, even the light image of consciousness, can be shown to be made up of strings.

It's time to back up a little bit, into the initial dimensions of space. Space is a positive dimensional aspect of the mirror image of itself, we can call the sub-space dimension. Sub-space is the inversional dimension of space (inside out space). Sub-space is where anti-matter exists, just as matter exists in our spacial dimension. Imaginational images, and dreams utilize sub-spacial dimensions as their playgrounds.

An entire universe exists in the sub-spacial dimension. As we shall soon discover, many universes, or realities can exist in the sub-spacial dimension simultaneously, just as they can in the spacial dimension of consciousness in our reality-they are linked.

Another entire unique universe exists within the sub-spacial dimension. It is an inverted anti-matter universe similar to our own, but with opposite quantum energy properties. Sub-spacial dimension is a parallel universe to our material universe, as we shall explore later in this string theory discussion.

Quantum physics CPT symmetry theory indicates that a subspace dimension with anti-matter would be a mirror image of our spacial reality. Imagination and other consciousness sentient spacial dimensions entangle through life from the spacial dimensions, into sub-spacial, anti-matter dimensions simultaneously as natural aspects of reality. It is part of what allows consciousness to exist in reality. Consciousness is without physical form, and without end according to the dictionary.

Imagination, and its dream visions are observed in the sub-spacial dimension, by means of quantum entanglement of the energized electrons moving through microtubules conduits running between billions of brains neurons, entangled into an activated Penial gland, located in the center of the human brain being approximately the size of a grain of rice-wow. Insight and other ideas are found in this dimension through intent of the individual, while meditating or just spacing out in a daydream. Third eye activation is sought after by millions of individuals worldwide, and has been for centuries. Meditation practices to activate the Penial gland are undertaken by millions worldwide, as spiritual practices.

String theory is satisfied to exist mathematically with at least 11 spacial dimensions, and acceptance of energy strings (light) being the foundational building blocks of our reality.

Quantum mechanics is appeased with bundles of strings creating subatomic particles, allowing elements of matter to combine in endless configurations to create reality through the entanglement of energy into matter.

Relativity is appeased with stabilized relationships between dimensions, relative to each other $E=MC^2$. The equation Einstein discovered indicates that energy can be converted into mass, while mass can be converted into energy. It takes a lot of energy to make a little mass, and only a little mass to make a lot of energy. Each entangled dimension is appeased with its assigned function creating a working productive reality, for observation and experience of living consciousness.

The quantum physics multi-verse (many worlds) theory is appeased as each living observer perceives a different, and unique reality in their consciousness, observation of it. Quantum mechanics (many worlds) actually allows 10^{500} alternate realities to exist simultaneously, with mathematical proofs to back the theories fantastic parameters.

Quantum physics dictates that the observation determines the experimental outcome. Once an observation is conducted, the state of the experimental subject becomes closed, or defined. Before any observation is conducted, the subject of the experiment is open to any conclusional results.

Each spacial dimension can be traced down to existing as a result of infinitely small strings of energy entangling directly, or indirectly to create our reality, with time and space being byproducts of realities existence.

The scientific Holographic Principle (a reality theory) agrees, and entangles within this string theory framework of reality. The Holographic principle states that reality is a three-dimensional projection made up of light pixels. Both theories state that reality is basically constructed from pixels of light energy at its foundational levels.

With the entanglement of consciousness into the sub-spacial dimension, all consciousness theoretically could entangle on a deep subconscious level. The sub-spacial environment where all consciousness can entangle is given different names in different books of thought. Historically deep thinkers like Einstein, and Tesla among others, have claimed to retrieve ideas and information through insightful meditation with conscious intent to do so.

All different life forms species experience reality through given methods, with unique perspectives to consciously record reality, (entangle memories) with the universal imagination in sub-space. (Akashic Record) being available for higher life forms with advance consciousness faculties, (human) pondering. Some religious texts call it the book of life.

The information paradox theory (a black hole theory) states that around any black hole, singularity, at its event horizon, all information that passes through its field (event horizon) will be stored by natural means. The information will also be retrievable at later time by natural means of technology. Many humans have apparently utilized this natural information technology for many years to date, as revealed by inventions, and testimonies. We will eventually tie this dimensional aspect of the event horizon information paradox to the Akashic Record (book of life) touched on above. More on this discussion later, when the quantum mechanics of the gravity well, black hole event horizon, information storage system is analyzed. I like to call it a time cast spell, gravity well.

Looking at reality through the eyes of string theory we can see how our multidimensional reality is assembled, allowing us as conscious living beings to experience a deep and full life of observational and interactive entanglement (intentive behavior), within our multidimensional reality. This giving rise to emotions and limitless imagination, which we can become immersed within. Conscious interactivness to experience life, is our assigned activity in this reality. (The meaning of life).

As humanity continues to evolve and create, we will discover continuously advancing abilities, drawing us deeper and deeper into realities wondrous gifts, of conscious entanglement, while interacting with reality and its amazing experiences.

In the discussion of String Theory and deeper physics which it encompasses, one inevitably encounters the difficult fact, that consciousness becomes involved on an entangled dimensional level, which must be addressed in order to proceed deeper into it with validity. Quantum physics dictate that experimental observation determines experimental outcome, and closes any system being observed, so the consciousness, which observes' reality, must be analyzed.

The holographic principle regarding singularities states that the entropy of mass (including black holes) is proportional to surface area, that volume itself is illusory, and the universe is really a hologram which is isomorphic to the information on the surface of its boundary (Event Horizon).

Consider then that each individual observes reality from their own unique perspective. Even a simple phrase can be interpreted in many way, such as "we are created in god's image", for instance. One individual may perceive this statement to mean that we look like god. Another individual may perceive it to mean that god is dreaming about us, in Gods mind. And another individual may perceive the statement to mean that we were created with some of god's attributes, like emotions or ethics. Another may say we look like God, but smaller.

All of the perceiving individuals has interpreted the statement correctly, at least as far as understanding the words by definition, contained in the statement (communication). Even with correct interpretation, many different, yet correct understandings may be perceived. It then becomes the perceived observation, to which the observer becomes entangled within. Reality can become complex for the thinking individual. Reality can be exciting for the participating individual who is enthusiastically involved (entangled).

In the many sentient dimensions of consciousness, we are able to access the sub spacial dimension of imagination, the dimension where dreams occur, or are created. When immersed into a good dream, the consciousness can believe that dream is the actual reality, while being unaware of the material reality the body is sleeping within, until waking up from the dream. When you awaken, the dream is quickly forgotten most of the time.

Where is the reality, that the dream takes place in, or at? How is dreaming really distinguished from our material reality, in the consciousness? By an alarm clock? A dream that seems so real to you, allowing you to become immersed into it, and then you wake up suddenly, shocked. You want to go back to sleep to continue the dream, but usually cannot.

If your mind believed the dream was real, was it then real? Is time entangled into the conscious reality of the dream, and waking state of life? Is your waking state true reality? Does it seem so when you fall back to sleep for another dream? Think about and remember some of your reoccurring dreams, and how your mind reacts while experiencing the dreams you have had over and over again. Is this consciously perceived sub-spacial reality (Dreamland) just another relativity, quantum mechanical enigma?

Microbiology defines consciousness in part as the resulting process of electrons passing through the microtubules in the brain cells, as the energized electrons are in the process of quantum entanglement, (in more than one place simultaneously) it causes consciousness life to activate self-awareness. Consciousness required the entanglement of all spacial dimensions working in concert, with the many systems of a living body to provide the working platform for itself to exist. Consciousness is able to entangle throughout all spacial, and sub-spacial dimensions simultaneously, with the cooperation of the working body.

While entangled electrons in, and out of the human brain are couple by an active penial gland, and the visual cortex, humans experience dreams, visions, (hallucinations). The question is, where is the platform stage of the dream that is observed and experienced, complete with emotion, memories, communications, thinking, light, time, space, gravity, matter, a subconscious reality within our mind. Where is that view screen (alternate reality), (Virtual Reality) at, in your dream?

Sub consciousness removes our waking reality, leaving only imagination, and its suggested realities to work within the consciousness spacial dimension of imagination itself. It arises from entangled microtubule energized electron energy of consciousness, not of realities material spacial dimension. The human dream or hallucination is experienced in the subspace dimension of imagination, contained within consciousness of life within our material body. Imagine how time fits into space, yet remains a separate dimension which entangles within it, they are impregnated. All dimensions are impregnated within each other.

The visual cortex area of the brain, and penial gland engaged with the brains microtubules entangled energized electrons, are responsible for this overall entanglement procedure layer upon layer upon layer, dimensions entangle within dimensions, fractal layers of each dimension combined in quantum bundles, which create consciousness, and all of its spawned sentient spacial dimensions cooperating for the experience of itself (consciousness through material life). String theory's revealed multidimensional reality, relativity's unified field theory, then becomes unified but more complex, than a single unified theory could imply or explain in singularity. A set of unified field theories will surface containing each dimensional aspect of reality relative to strings and relative quantum science, once the mathematicians are able to proof out the enormous task at hand.

All life is conscious, proof of consciousness, and its ability of entanglement become more evident in bacteria which is being observed worldwide. The bacteria continue to grow in resistance to antibiotics, despite locality of interactions to defeat them. The bacteria display entangled intelligence, with the ability to communicate over large distances to survive new antibiotic attack. Despite the separation of continents, the bacteria are able to alter its own DNA to survive the anti-biotic assault. Bacteria adapts to new antibiotics without having come into direct contact with them, due to entangled communication (sub-spacial) within its own species. This instinctual defense is a natural sentient spacial dimensional behavior response of living consciousness entangled into its own DNA operating system.

Quantum entanglement of energized electrons within the nervous systems of plant, animals and humans produces an electrical field which surrounds the material body of each living species. This field can be photographed by means of Kirllian photography, which was accidentally discover in the 1700ś. The electromagnetic field surrounding the individual life forms appears as a ghostly, aura, in a Kirllian photograph.

In plants this quantum entanglement process occurs within the photosynthesis process of converting light into energy. In other words, plants convert light into a kind of consciousness, by means of chemistry.

In animals and humans this occurs within the microtubules conduits in the living brain. A technical process know now as Kirllian photography shows this phenomenon on film as a light aura surrounding the body of any living species. It looks like a ghost when viewed in modified visible light which allows observation of its (consciousness) reality, or verification of the conscious entangled energy field. By definition consciousness is without material body, and without end from death.

Consciousness is the combined entanglement of many systems working in concert to give rise to life, and allowing conscious observation, which additional parametrical dimensions, such as emotion, imagination, thinking, communication, memory, and learning combine which enrich the experience, as life evolves into the future of reality through time.

This also verifies that consciousness is within the body, and also separate from the body in a simultaneous symbiotic manner. When adding the entanglement of the other sentient dimensions such as emotion, thought, memory, communication, imagination, and spirituality, it become clearer that there is a lot more to a living being than just a material body. Part of the definition of consciousness, is without material body.

This gives rise to amplified spirituality, and therefor religion follows natural evolution in our species as a synthetic dimension. Religion advances spirituality into a tangible institution with rules and specific guidelines of membership (governmental aspects). Religion give individuals something to work towards and gather in groups for, socializing. Further deepening the living experience for individuals in each cultural segment of humanity. Basically, all religions have more in common than not, behaviorally speaking. Each dimension entangles with each other dimension, to make up more than the sum of their parts. One plus two equals three, in this string theory reality.

Consciousness of all life species on the planet earth are then entangled on at least a basic level of existence. Think of the trillions of cells in a single human body. The estimated eighty-six trillion cells, each contain hundreds of mitochondria, which are the energy centers of all cells, regardless of cell functioning properties. In other words, bone cells, stomach cells, and brain cells all have specific functioning's. The mitochondria function the same way in all of the cells throughout the body, regardless of cell functional assignments. The hundreds of mitochondria in each cell are symbiotic hosts to the body, but work to ensure its ongoing life, without regard to assignments.

Bundles of cooperating cells work in groups as different aspects of the body to ensure continuing life and correct functioning, throughout one lifetime. The DNA previously assigned each cell to grow into the required functioning organs or systems to ensure proper bodily functioning, liver cells, muscle cells, bone cells, etc. The brain and nervous systems coordinate cellular activity throughout the body. The DNA command each cell to grow into task specific working cells, in every living species. All consciousness relies on the cooperation of multiple working parameters, within its dimensional scope, to function as a living being with purpose to observe and experience reality, while being entangled within the sum of its parts. The individual cells cooperate with the DNA instruction, while performing assigned duties, allowing a symbiotic relationship, which ensures the foundation for living consciousness to thrive inside of the material body host.

None of the separate body parts is aware of the others, or their interaction to provide sentient life for the entire organism. In a symbiotic concert, each does its part to create the living conscious human being, animal, or plant. In the same fractal dynamic, each human is a symbiotic host to the human collective, unaware of its big picture contribution, each human does what they do to assist in human progress. Reality is the summations of all living consciousness entangled within twenty-eight spacial dimensions, composed of tiny vibrating string of energy which give substance to everything we be and see. This discussion is me, helping the technology dimension be more than anyone can see.

In the same fractal dynamic process, each species on planet earth contributes to the food chain, and other aspects of the living planet to which they are unaware. Example-(bees cross pollinating plants), (Plankton feeding the larger oceans species). The planet is then able to host over seven million separate living conscious species. None of the living species is aware of its contribution to the entire living organism we call earth, (Gia) yet each contributes as required without question.

The consciousness level of the different species may vary in depth, and parameters utilized, but conscious they are. It is unlikely that plants experience imagination, or that insects can think. It is likely that humans are at the top of the earthly evolutionary system in that we have access to more spacial dimensions that other species on the planet. The planet is then a symbiotic multidimensional working sentient consciousness of its own, as it evolves in time, to change and improve itself through cooperative relationships around, and within the world it hosts.

On another larger fractal level, we see the solar system, and even galaxies evolving in similar manners as symbiotic host to larger and larger entities, which we must assume contain consciousness on some levels, as a matter of observation.

Black holes in galaxies which assist with recycling, and gravitational stabilities. Event horizons which are storing information for retrieval by intelligence species through imagination or meditation, other technologies may exist to accomplish this also. Other planets which can host life and consciousness. Planets with advanced life whom choose to spread out in the galaxy by means of technological superiority.

Think about plankton in the ocean which feed whales, and small fish. Stars making light so that life can initiate and evolve. Asteroid impacts with planets can affect terraforming, and chemistry alterations in the impacted planets evolutionary timeline. Asteroids and comets which can provide raw materials for intelligent species to construct with. None of the individual entities is aware of their purpose in the larger picture of reality. In Spirituality the imagined creator God is the only consciousness which could possibly understand, and create such a reality, in which this discussion is entering.

When we consider that our universe was created from nothing more than a bunch of Hydrogen and Helium fourteen billion years ago, when the big bang explosion initiated the universe (matter based reality) it seems rather amazing, that we end up here. Just to think about this is a worthwhile experience for our living consciousness, and emotional sentient spacial dimensional selves, not to mention the spiritual implications created within the thought itself.

For every particle of matter there must exist a mirror image particle of anti-matter, basic physics. Many of the universal anti-matter particles exist in an entangled state of being. Anti-matter exists in our material reality for a millisecond before flashing off (encountering a matter particle) or entangling back into its own sub-spacial dimension. The remaining anti-matter to balance our reality matter, is contained within the sub-spacial dimension. An entire universe within itself, from our perspective.

Quantum mechanics CPT Theory allows time to flow backwards in anti-matter sub spacial dimensions in some observational situations. Does a particle in an entangled anti-matter state go back in time until returning back to the spacial dimension as matter, which would allow time to be ignored, for particles/anti-particles in each dimension by entangling?

Reverse time in anti-matter subspace allows entangled particles to be here and there simultaneously, without wasting time or energy according to CPT symmetry theory, its quantum solution satisfies relativity. Relative time anyways.

Imagination is a sentient spacial dimension impregnated within consciousness, just as a movie disk, is shown on the television screen. Imagination allows free will of mental image creation within living consciousness. Dreams as realistic as reality; to the dreamer. Focused imagination can create alternative realities. Quantum mechanics allows 10^{500} alternate realities to simultaneously exist. Many worlds theory allows 10^{500} realities at the same time, wow. Each individual is able to create a reality (imagination, dream) within their conscious imagination, which fits the theory of many worlds, interpretation wise and according to mathematical science, when viewed from this observational reference perspective.

Each individual, observes a unique reality within their living consciousness, as interpretation is experienced from individual perspectives. In other words, your world is a little bit different than my world. Think about crime witness statements to the investigators, who are trained to assemble only the like statements from the group of witnesses and victims, in order to make sense of the facts involved. Each testimony varies from the others due to perspective observations of the individuals, just as each of us observes a slightly different reality within our consciousness, even while observing identical experiences. Many worlds simultaneously, many individuals observing simultaneously. Your dog and cat observe reality from different perspectives alike. Even your houseplants experience some extent of reality through their nervous systems, air temperature, electrical charges, and moisture content in the air. Most plants respond favorably to soft music also. Many worlds theory is gaining weight in our technologically evolving society. String theory along with the holographic principle also fit in with this line of thought when the observer opens up to the relative reality in which this discussion finds itself, a quantum enigma of sorts, depending on acceptance of perspective observational conclusions. Proofs on this level of thinking seem unattainable, yet disputation of the theories implied possibly just as much.

Within imagination, time, space, matter, light, gravity, mathematics, communication, technology, and life in motion (reality) can and does exist to the observer creator of the imaginational daydreaming reflections.

Remember daydreaming through boring lecture in school as a child. Remember your pet cat staring into space, in contentment, just sitting there daydreaming about something it liked. Dreaming is imagination in full activity as the subconscious mind is at the forefront. Imagination is when consciousness has intent to pursue an idea, situation, or a memory. They are the same sentient spacial dimensional accessing point within the living consciousness.

When dreaming in the spacial dimension of imagination, time can seem to flow in a very different rate, than it does in waking consciousness states. Time flows in our spacial dimension, one way, and in imagination another way. Sub-spacial time may be observed in reverse according to quantum mechanics theories-based deductions.

Often upon awakening from a long dream, we realize the entire dream has been experienced in a couple of minutes or less, on the alarm clock scale. This confirms that time is relative to the observer, and the state of mind that the observer is in, at the time of the observations.

Certain drugs can distort temporal awareness of time passing also, by means of chemistry. Time is relatively compressible in the sub-spacial dimension, which does not conflict with relativity regulations of temporal behavior. Absolute time is the only law breaker in our reality.

The comparison of consciousness, to spirit can be used to relay the concept of eternal life from spirituality to scientific physics. Many religions, promise eternal life in paradise in their sales pitches, as a possibility to worthy individuals. Can a correlation be made with consciousness, imagination, and eternal conscious awareness scientifically?

The laws of thermodynamics state that energy cannot be destroyed, energy can change forms. With respect to these thoughts, is then reincarnation a deductive process of life? Consciousness by definition is without the body, without end. The body sleeps while the consciousness is off on wild dreaming adventures which seem as real as reality itself. Consciousness does not require sleep; but the body does require sleep. The body requires energy to live. Consciousness is the energy of life.

Energize electrons made of subatomic strings being entangled from matter to anti matter without the expense of time. Conscious imagination creating a unique reality for each observer. Dreams occurring without effort, while the practiced imaginer creates unique internal realities (Virtual Realities) within an empty conscious mind. How can science explain this accommodation? Mental astral projection. Third eye visual development.

> Ezekiel 1:1; "The heavens were opened, and I saw visions of God."

God is said to be a spirit creature, who abides in the unseen realm of heaven. Did Ezekiel and all of the other blessed individuals, get a divine visit within their imaginations, sub-spacial dimensional access? God wants us to communicate with him, does God not? Dimensions where god resides, subspace spacial dimension which entangles with human conscious imagination. Maybe, maybe not? Do we have the absolute ability to say yes, or no to this query? Thinking individuals may enjoy this line of posturing. Exercise the mind, grow strong.

Singularities - Black Hole Centers

Black holes in space are created when large stars deplete their fuel, and then collapse as gravitational forces overcome the counteracting nuclear fusions' attempts to support the star, forcing the dyeing star to bounce back after total collapse as it explodes its outer shell away. The remaining star matter gravitationally falls into itself with exceptional gravitational force. The remaining collapsing star matter can form a black hole, if sufficient matter is remaining, after the supernova.

The gravitational forces of sufficiently large collapsing stars cause a large portion of the remaining materials to get compressed into an extreme state of density, beyond that of a Neutron star. Within the Neutron star the electrons and protons have been squashed into neutrons, and are packed together so tight that there is no space between the Neutrons. Neutron stars are known to have matter densities of over a hundred thousand metric tons per cubic centimeter. That is an incomprehensible amount of density, not observable in our direct reality. Theoretically the Neutron star is the densest object understood by known physics. Black holes are denser yet, than Neutron stars.

A black hole is the densest object that we can indirectly detect, in this reality. The black hole resulting from a large collapsed star has gravitational forces strong enough to keep even light from escaping its grasp, thereby making it impossible to observe directly. To be denser than a Neutron star the sub-atomic matter must behave in a way not yet understood by human sciences. Infinities arise in the relivity mathematics at singularity. Infinities in mathematics mean that we do not understand the conclusional formulas correctly.

Black holes are known to be abundant in the universe. Every galaxy we observe contains a massive black hole at its center, which assists with gravitational cohesion for the galaxy. These massive black holes can range from four million solar masses, like the one in the center of our galaxy, to four billion solar masses. Additional black holes are also scattered throughout the galaxies, possibly numbering in the millions for each galaxy. Accurate count of black holes is difficult due to the fact that they appear as invisible black places in the blackness of space, when looked for. They can be indirectly detected presently by observing objects, and accretion disks, or other stars and planets orbiting around black holes in space.

Mathematics completed by a mathematician years ago dictated that a star of sufficient size, could collapse into a single point in space, (singularity) due to extreme gravitational forces upon itself. The Chandrasekhar limit was established, for stars with solar masses at least three times that of our own sun. When such a star collapses at its grand finally, it is thought to collapse in on itself until it is confined to an infinitely small point in space, called a Singularity. We have not been able to verify this phenomenon for various reasons. It doesn't happen very often in human life span frequency. The singularity gravity bends its own light back in on itself, rendering itself invisible.

The entire black hole (thousands of times more massive than earth) being squashed down to the size of a single point in space seems absurd to many. The mathematics are correct, but that is not to say that the entire collapsing star ends up in the singularity. A section of the mathematics creates infinities at singularity. Infinities basically tell us that something unexplainable occurs.

Perhaps only some of the collapsing star is squashed hard enough to end up in the (singularity), and the rest piles up around it in layers. The singularity may be encapsulated within a neutron star density outer core. Most other celestial bodies are composed of layers of increasing density approaching their centers.

That would mean that the actual singularity was at the core of the black hole, and other less dense material such as Neutron star material (Neutrons tightly packed together, with no orbiting electrons) could be the next layer out from the singularity. This configuration would have the gravitational potential to prevent light from escaping, and fulfill other requirements of this discussions parameters. With the largest of black holes an even less dense outer layer might be at white dwarf star density level. The combined gravity of the multi layered object would still have the ability to bend its own light back into itself, and harbor an event horizon.

The event horizon is the imaginary spherical boundary surrounding a singularity from which the gravity is still strong enough to prevent light from leaving the singularities surrounding area. That is why the singularity is called a black hole. When viewed from afar there is no light to observe, only a black hole in space.

Any matter object that gets within the event horizons spherical plane will be gravitationally drawn into the singularity, to be consumed. Black holes feed on anything that comes close enough to be gravitationally attracted to them. When a black hole feeds on enough matter (a lot of matter), in a short period of time it becomes voracious, ejecting powerful gamma, and x-ray jets from its polar apexes, at near the speed of light. These high energy waste fountains can reach millions of light years into deep space, as the black hole feeds itself.

These jets are among the most energetic phenomenon that have ever been witnessed by humans. If one of these jets were to hit the earth, from a distance of less than five hundred light years, our atmosphere would likely be stripped away from the planet, and all life in its path eradicated within seconds. These jets seem to occur when the black hole attempts to eat more than it can digest. Gravity of the singularity does not discriminate, it just pulls any trespassing object or matter into itself. Consider the super massive black holes in galactic centers to be the top predators of the universal food chain of reality.

The event horizon surrounding the black hole is the point of no return for anything attempting to enter. The event horizon works both ways, as it does not allow anything to leave the black hole from the inside either. The only exception is the cosmic gamma and x-ray jets it expels through polar apexes when voraciously feeding. The magnetic polar apexes allow high energy matter expulsion, like a pressure relief valve. The event horizon forms a barrier from the inside, as its gravity prevents the light from escaping the singularity.

The detained light within the event horizon forms a light energy barrier, which is thought to act as an information storage device. The information paradox theory indicates that any information (matter) passing the event horizon field is stored on its surface. If we could look at the event horizon from within its spherical radius, it might look like a very bright mirrored, metallic surface (frozen light). From the outside it would look like a dull black smooth surface.

A scientific theory called the information paradox states that any matter entering the black hole deposits all of its information onto the event horizon surface, which can then be retrieved by natural means. The information retrieval method has not yet been scientifically determined. Black holes are far away, and unapproachable by current technology levels.

This theory states that the event horizon stores all information that passes through it, like a computer disk. Speculation into the information storage parameters vary. One thought is that the information is stored on a two-dimensional digital format, like a television screen picture. The universe may have a memory storage system, the function of a singularity's event horizon, which might be superior to the living consciousness memory we experience.

There are individuals who believe the information stored on the event horizon is accessible by means of entangled imagination or insight. Quantum Entanglement occurs in quantum mechanics without penalty of time, over any distance without energy conservation issues.

Many great thinkers throughout history stated that they received information while daydreaming or pondering a topic. Einstein, Tesla, and many others alike. Others call this information library the Akashic Record. Religious books might call it the book of life. Adam and Eve read the forbidden book of knowledge in the garden. Regardless, it would seem that insight through imagination allows for information transfer to living consciousness in humans in a selective manner. More on the entanglement feature of singularities and event horizons later in this discussion.

Black holes devour entire star systems, and anything living within the detainment gravitational zone, just like animal predators eat other animals. Black holes also eat each other from time to time. A logical deduction would then be that when one black hole consumes another, the information stored on its event horizon would then be stored on the consuming black holes event horizon, so the information and its energy would not be lost, in accordance with the laws of conservation of energy.

The event horizon surrounding singularities distorts time and space around the gravity well. The singularity creates a deep space gravity well according to Einstein's relativity mathematics. Someone falling into the event horizon from an outside observer's point of view, would seem to become frozen in time at the event horizon surface. But to the faller, falling into the event horizon would be a continuous fall into the singularity, out of sight of any outside observer, from the faller's perspective, it's all relative, in relativity.

The falling object, would however be elongated and then spaghettified from the singularities intensive gravity, as it approached. The spaghettified atom stream would deposit all of its information onto the event horizon information storage system as it passed through its invisible boundary. The falling object would become nothing more than a stream of atoms as it entered the singularity, and then would impact the black hole surface with incredible motion (inertial) energy. After passing though the event horizon.

We can only speculate on the composition of the black hole since its gravity prevents light from escaping its event horizon. The only thing we can observe when looking at a black hole is the empty space that the event horizon allows us to observe. We can observe the cosmic gamma, x-ray jets that are ejected from the black holes polar apexes, when it is in its voracious feeding mode. We can also detect orbiting stars circling the black void in space, and deduce the presents of the black hole by its gravitational effects. We can now detect gravity waves emanating from black hole collisions. With mathematics and gravitational observations, we can determine the estimated mass of the indirectly observable black hole.

As for the composition of the black hole, we can speculate by logical deduction. We know that collapsed stars of medium size usually end up as white dwarf stars, which have average densities of thousands of tons per cubic centimeter. At that density, a sugar cubes worth of white dwarf star matter, held in your hand would fall through your hand, hit the ground, and punch a hole right through the planet until it reached the central core.

Larger stars collapse into neutron stars who have average densities of hundreds of thousands of tons per cubic centimeter. Neutron stars are matter compressed so tight that all of their electron and protons have been squashed into more neutrons. It is believed that these neutrons are packed together so tight that they are touching each other. In comparison normal atoms contain hundreds of thousands of time more space than solid atomic matter. Neutron stars are the densest matter humans are aware of, that is visible.

We also know that singularities are denser than neutron stars. We deduce this from the fact that neutron stars are visible, and singularities are not. Singularities form when very large stars collapse onto themselves. These phenomena occur when the mass of the collapsing star exceeds the Chandrasekhar limit, which states mathematically that the collapsing body will continue to collapse until its matter occupies a single point in space, with all of its mass in tacked. This immense matter phenomenon then creates the black hole that we are unable to directly observe. The mathematics surrounding singularities end in conclusion at infinities, meaning something strange is occurring at singularity.

Singularity gravitational forces are at the theoretical limit which the universe allows. Super massive black holes get around this by simply growing much larger in spherical size than ordinary black holes, and are found at most galaxies center, where finding food to consume for growth is usually not a problem.

It has been speculated that some of the singularities radiation should leak away from the event horizon, like an evaporation effect, and should be detectable by some means around the event horizon edge. This evaporation process would allow the black hole to bleed off its energy (Hawkins Radiation) eventually allowing the black hole to completely evaporate into space as energy. This process is thought to take more time than the universe has been in existence so far to proceed to end. This is theoretical physics at its best, with mathematic proofs to allow its safe predictions.

Stephen Hawkins is perhaps the greatest mathematician, and physicist that I have ever read about, and watched on the television. His theories have inspired me to take up theoretical physics as a lifelong hobby, as well as a natural curiosity. His zest for life and physics inspires me, as well as thousands of others to work harder, and never stop trying to improve on what we believe in, and can learn from each other.

As we think about the black hole, singularities composition, knowing that it is denser than a neutron star, and that the neutron star is composed of tightly pack neutrons, which almost have enough gravity to hold light in, but not quite. I then think about how stars are composed of layers of matter in increasingly dense composition approaching their centers. Planets and galaxies are composed in similar fashions. Extrapolating, while thinking about the larger picture of reality, and string theory, I imagine the singularity composed in the same layered fashion.

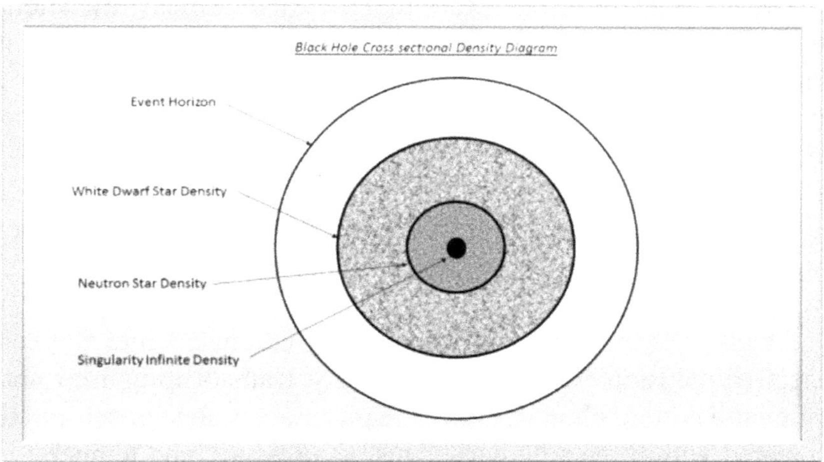

A black hole that is composed in increasingly dense layers moving towards it center (singularity) would not detract from the Chandrasekhar limit collapsing into a single point in space. Imagine that the large star collapses, as suggested in the Chandrasekhar mathematics, and a portion of it does collapse into the singularity, where a new state of matter now exists within it. This matter would be more compact than a neutron star, with compacted neutrons being entangled into each other, creating entangled super-matter.

The packed Neutrons would begin to overlap each other's residing spaces, merging together. Gravity fighting to squeeze the super entangled matter even tighter, creating heat and nuclear repulsion forces to compensate for the extreme pressures. The packing Neutrons fight to separate from merging, but are overpowered by gravity as they converge into each other.

Imagine a point where the neutron stars gravitational center (singularity) then became a new state of matter which was much denser than anything else in reality, (Neutrons converging in space together, two becoming, one, compressing beyond infinity) while bending space and time so hard that they just collapse reality, into singularity.

The matter surrounding the singularity remains in the neutron star density state, pushing inward into the singularities gravitational center, pushing ever harder into the entangled super-matter from its gravitational obedience. The singularities entangled super-matter is being forced inward on itself without mercy, and yet cannot be forced any further, in the spacial dimension. The increasing nuclear forces within, will not allow particle escape. The entangled super-matter at the singularity center point is in a stale mate with reality, and its most powerful forces, gravity pushing the matter pressure and density levels into infinities.

At infinity the dense super-matter is entangled into the sub-spacial dimension while simultaneously transforming into anti-matter as a natural phenomenon of reality. A new state of sub-matter is created within the singularity. Just as pressure, and temperature cause matter to transform from gas into liquids, and solids. Pressure and temperature also transform solids into neutron matter, and into inverted matter, or anti-matter.

Imagine the gravitational forces being great enough at the singularity point to force the matter from space into the sub-spacial dimension by means of entanglement transformation. The singularities gravity, pressure, and temperature transform the matter into anti-matter, and into the sub-spacial dimension simultaneously, by means of natural phenomenon. In other words, the matter within the singularity is transformed into anti-matter, and into the sub-spacial dimension as a result of three extreme dimensional forces which have reached mathematical infinities.

This would solve the infinity equational results that relativity comes up with at singularity, with respect to mass density results. The infinity result could then be verified, as the densely packed entangling super-matter at singularity, is no longer in the spacial dimension (single point in space). It has been leaked (been forced) into sub-space while transferring its material properties to anti-matter as a result of the dimensional transformation shift.

This newly transformed anti-matter could then account for the (Hawkins Radiation) which is thought to allow the black hole to eventually evaporate over billions of years, completing their life cycles. The difference is, that in this model, the Hawkins Radiation leaks (transforms or entangles) into the singularities center point, into the sub-space dimension, instead of away from its event horizon into spacial dimension.

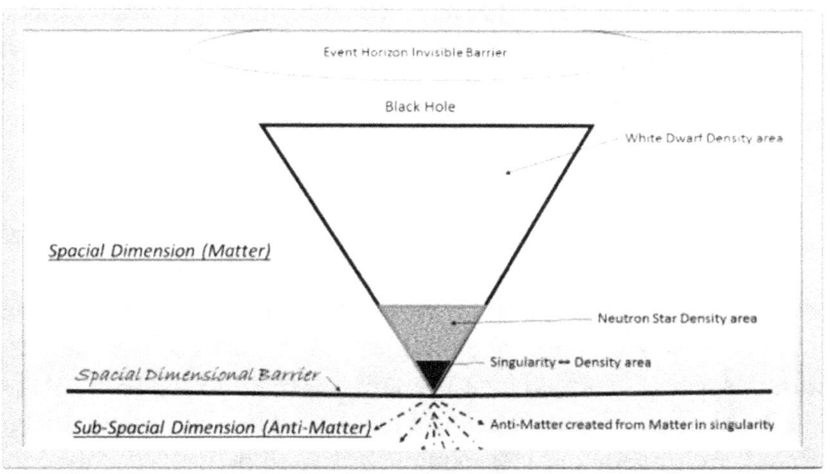

In the bigger picture of reality with respect to string theory, this phenomenon would also allow the explanation, of how the initial universal matter in the big bang was created. It is thought that the matter in our universe was all created from pure energy at the time of the big bang. All of the matter in the universe created at one time, at one point in space, really? Sounds like a big stretch to me.

All of the matter in the universe is said to have spontaneously appeared in the moment of the big bang. That's a lot of matter, when we consider the trillion galaxies which the Hubble telescope can now detect, in its ultra-deep field study, containing around a hundred billion stars each, with about ten planets each, not counting moons, asteroids, comets and nebulous gas clouds, right! All of the matter in the universe coming from a single point in space, really? Trillions of galaxies. I need another explanation than that please, my mind can't get a hold on that.

Later on that, for now let's keep the discussion on the singularities, black holes, and event horizons. The universe needs to recycle energy and matter in ways which allow it to self-sustain, whether we understand them or not. Human science calls it laws of conservation of energy.

Keeping all of the new ideas in mind, let's add another one to the mix. Within the event horizon, the information paradox theory states that all information entering into the event horizon will be save, stored, and retrievable. Thinking back to the sub-spacial dimensions of consciousness, imagination, thought, and memory. Imagine the event horizon entangling its stored information through the singularity, into the sub-spacial dimension simultaneously.

This would be similar to the process of the living consciousness entangling energized electron within the brain, and around the body at the same time. Imagine the living consciousness imagination being able to access event horizon entangled sub-spacial information as a natural aspect of reality. Hang in there, we're almost in.

The Akashic Record (book of knowledge) or place where Insight is found, we understand it somehow. It is used by millions of people to acquire new ideas, technology, and inventions. Anything that humanity ever invented, was first a product of the imagination, and then required thought, and memory to initially create. We understand that our imaginations entangle into another dimension to create the images which we picture in our consciousness.

Now let's put the discussion into reverse gear. Let's imagine that the living consciousness's imagination is able to feed ideas, and thoughts into the Akashic Record naturally. Suppose we can receive, and send the information into the universal information storage system. This takes the discussion into a more realistic stance, as it balances the Akoshic informational (book of knowledge) transfer into a two-way street. "Anything man can dream, man can create" is written in one of those old religious books somewhere.

The black hole event horizon stores information, of everything that passes through its barrier. Accessible information to all conscious living species, as information or instincts. There are trillions of black holes in our universe. In time, everything around a black hole will pass through the event horizons barrier, as its gravity pull everything in its vicinity into itself for feeding, and digestion. The black hole exists, it feeds, and it stores information. It expels singularity matter into sub-spacial dimension as anti-matter, and also excretes spacial dimension matter waste by means of polar apex cosmic gamma and x-ray jets, after feeding enough. Does this make the black hole a living entity of sorts, a new species to our understanding? Keeping the mind open to new ideas again, there's more.

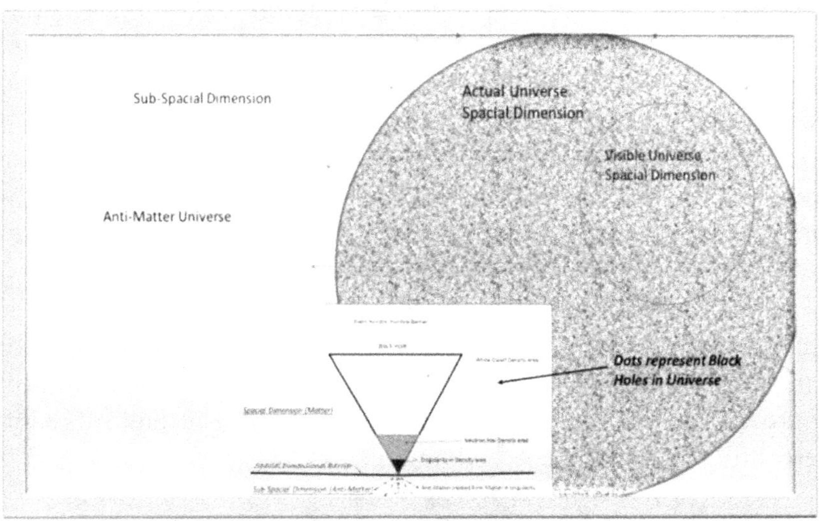

Extrapolating and expanding on the thoughts of one singularity entangling event horizon information into sub-spacial dimension;

to imagining all singularities entangling stored information into the sub-spacial dimension, entangling together as a natural function of reality.

Imagine all singularities acting like our living consciousness's human brains neurons, and synaptic system which entangle energized electrons into our living consciousness with imaginative, thinking, emotional, and memory abilities. Imagine all of the universal singularities entangling information through transition into sub-spacial dimensions while being conscious of said information flow. It is written in the religious texts that we are created in gods 'own image! God can hold the universe in his hand.

This gives new meaning to that statement does it not? All singularities entangling event horizon information bundles simultaneously. Trillions of singularities in our reality connected (entangled) into the sub-spacial dimension being consciously entangled, with information storage like brain neurons, a giant (beyond comprehension) living conscious universal mind of some kind.

Now keeping the aforementioned in memory for recall, while we think about our own human imaginational abilities. Our imaginations entangle into the event horizon information storage system (Akashic Record) or (book of knowledge) and the event horizon information storage system is but a single cell in another universal sentient life forms mind, on a massive fractal level, in the sub-spacial dimension. Are we then in contact with a sentient supreme being when we imagine, meditate, daydream or pray? In a two-way communication medium we could then directly give and take information.

Direct communication with said informational reality, implies some very interesting thinking points, with respect to our relationship with all of our reality. This discussion is designed to open thinking minds with new perspectives on reality, hence the title edge of reality. Were still going in deeper, so hang on.

Creation and Evolution Explained?

As scientists have deduced, our universe was created about fourteen billion years ago in the big band explosion. We deduce this from galactic observation in which we find galaxies moving away from each other in general. The point in time of the universal creation seems correct with respect to the galactic mathematical vector proofs, and with the evidential situation that we observe as our universal reality.

Edwin Hubble made the first telescopic observations of the galactic realities, which shocked humanity. His first revelation was the observation that our milky way was not the entire universe, but only one of thousands of galaxies in the visible universe. Until that time science considered the milky way galaxy to be the universe. Shattering that idea in itself made the world seem a lot smaller, and the universe a lot bigger.

His second revelation was that the galaxies which we can observe are moving away from us at high velocities, and the father away the galaxies are from earth, the faster they are moving away from it. That told humanity that its entire universe seemed to be expanding. The next revelation was that somehow the universal expansion was accelerating by means of an unknown phenomenon, we now call dark energy. It is a mystery that things as large as galaxies could be accelerated by a force, which apparently is spread out over the entire universe, yet remains unexplained. Many scientific papers have been written on the speculation of what dark energy might be.

All of the matter in the universe was then thought to have been created at the time of the big bang, from nothing. Cleaver mathematicians have provided plausible methods to explain this occurrence. Matter can be created from energy, just as energy can be created from matter. $E=MC^2$ allows for this.

If the matter was created initially from energy, and that is a lot of matter incidentally, trillions of galaxies containing billions of stars and planets, moons, asteroids, comets, gas clouds, etc. Where then did the energy come from to create all of that matter that we observe in the universe? That's a lot of energy, and matter any way you think about it.

In the same thought, we want to find out why the observations of the universal galaxies are showing a gravitational effect that requires very much more matter than we observe universally. Scientists have calculated that our universe would need about ten times the matter we estimate it has presently, to create the gravitational force required to continue its expansion, not to mention the accelerating expansion we observe.

Some of this acceleration gravitational effect can be explained by the observation of inflationary motion of the initial, and present-day actual universe, as explained earlier in this discussion.

Now to get things balanced out universally in this discussion, we need to decide what existed before the big bang event. If energy created the big bang explosion, where did it come from, and where did it reside? In this string theory discussion, we will assume that the anti-matter dimension existed before our material spacial dimension universe was created. A mirror universe to our own, filled with anti-matter instead of matter. A high energy event then occurred in the sub-spacial dimension which disrupted the sub-spacial dimension to the point of singularity. The resulting explosion in sub-space created a spacial dimension which rapidly expanded through sub-space with growing spherical boundaries which continues to expand presently. The sub-space dimension allows faster than light travel as a matter of its own relativity laws. The explosion in the sub-spacial dimension continues its expansion into the spacial dimension now.

Our universe is, and has been expanding into the sub-spacial dimension at two times the speed of light, as a result of the initial forces created in the big bang explosion fourteen billion years ago. This mathematically dictates that we have ten times more galaxies in the actual universe, than we have in the observable visible universe, which agrees with current gravitational observation estimates. How can a statement like that be made?

It is deduced by means of taking what is known, and what is observed, and making logical deductions from those. Since scientist wants there to be ten time more matter than we can observe in the universe, to explain dark energy's universal expansion effect. We know the universe initially expanded by means of inflation. That observation has lead scientists to deduce that something is causing the expansion beyond gravitational effects of known universal matter. It stands to reason that the universe initially expanded faster than light speed as a result of the explosion, and nothing (no space) to keep it from slowing down in its path.

Before the big bang there was no spacial dimension, no time, no matter. Relativity allows faster than light speed travel, if traveling in a non-spacial environment. When the big bang initially occurred there was no space, allowing the big bang explosion the ability to proceed away from its (center point), in a spherical expansion pattern at twice the speed of light (inflation), because there was no space in front of it, to hold it back (relativity limit), only sub-spacial anti matter.

With the universe expanding at twice the speed of light, we can calculate that it contains ten times the amount of space and matter that we can observe in the visible universe, due to relativity factors of visual regulation with respect to velocity. With ten times the space in the universe, it stands to reason that there would also be ten times the number of galaxies (matter) in the actual universe than there is in the visible universe. That accounts for some of the gravitational galactic expansion phenomena which we can observe, but not the acceleration of said galaxies.

Another way in which physicists explain the initial big bang explosion is, that another dimensional membrane bumped into our spacial membrane to create this universe. However, this would require our spacial universe to have existed before the big bang explosion, and would negate a lot of our present-day laws of physics, or at least the explanation that these laws were developed during the initial moments of the big bang, as was space and time itself.

Another plausible explanation might be, that in the sub-spacial dimension, where anti-matter is most prevalent (99.9%) that something unique occurred. An experiment, or some natural high energy phenomenon occurred within the sub-spacial dimension.

The sub-spacial dimension would have been much older than we can imagine at the time of the big bang explosion, it stands to reason in this discussion. This explosion created a new spacial dimension, from the sub-spacial perspective, then continued to grow in spherical size. Think of a big bomb exploding in outer space, it makes a spherical pattern.

From the sub-space dimension, it looked like an expanding ball of light, bright, glowing like a star, with lightning flashes occurring as it ripped uncontrollably into the sub-spacial dimension at twice the speed of light. Think of a bomb going off in our spacial dimension as you observe it, all you observe is a light flash, and then a shock wave. This was what our universe might have look like as it expands in the sub-spacial dimension.

Anti-matter was being converted into matter at the (explosions) bow shock wave front (Nexus wave) as it simultaneously transformed into the newly created spacial dimension that we reside in now. The speed at which this explosion continues to expand into sub-space dimension remains constant, as space is not governed by the light speed limit (c) while moving into sub-space. As it grows into sub-space, while expanding our spacial dimensional size, it transforms all anti-matter that gets caught in its way into matter. The newly created matter is the matter we observe in our reality.

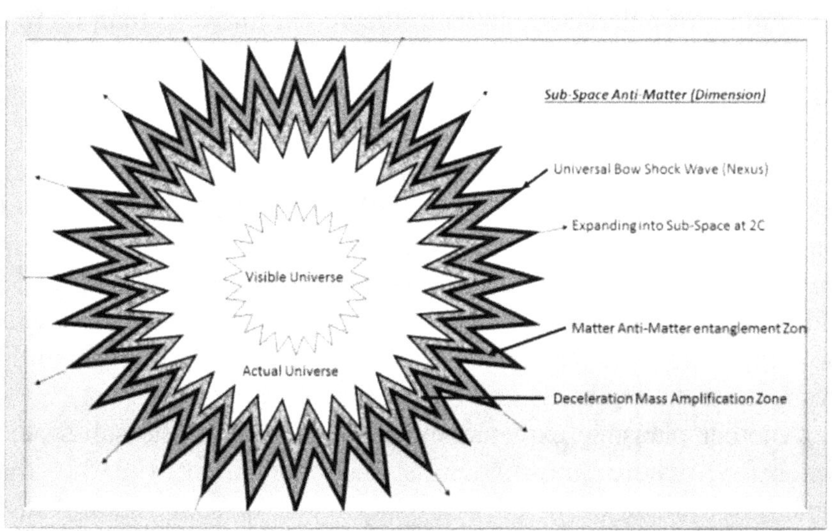

That also explains why the matter in our universe is so spread out and evenly developed. As this cataclysmic fireball continues to race into the sub-spacial dimension, its bow shock wave front transforms all anti-matter in front of it into matter, which is then in the spacial dimension as a result of being in the wrong spot at the right time. The sub-spacial dimension anti-matter stars and planets that get caught in the path of this big bang explosion wave front are instantly transformed into their opposite composition from anti-matter into matter. Moving from one dimension to another is the result of the Nexus wave front, relativity enigma which results.

This newly transformed matter then coalesces again through gravitational forces, and a relativity, which is occurring within the Nexus bow shock wave of the expanding universe, into the planets and stars we observe in our spacial dimension.

The bow shock wave front tearing into sub-space spherically, creating the spacial dimension is moving at twice the speed of light at its outermost perimeter. This velocity creates a Nexus wave front of energized matter, anti-matter phase transition shell, which results in additional gravitational entanglement of mass amplified inertial matter creation, which effects all matter within our spacial dimension, in different ways.

This spherical outer perimeter Nexus wave front of the spacial dimension impacts anti-matter particles in sub-space at twice the speed of light. This instantly phase transforms the anti-matter into matter particles, which are immediately then bound by relativity laws of physics.

These newly transformed matter particles are immediately enveloped into space moving past them at twice the speed of light. This creates an inverted, mass inertial amplified particle, as it now obtains infinite mass, while inverting due to relativity laws which states, that at high velocities matters length is reduced in direction of travel, while increasing mass to infinity. The particles which are traveling that much faster than light speed, (relatively) become inverted converting anti-matter into matter instantaneously. They naturally resist the transitional forces being applies, but transform non the less.

Even though the particles themselves are caught in the Nexus wave, and may be stationary initially (in sub-space dimension), the fact that space is moving past them at twice light speed, creates the same situation (relativity) high speed motion. Whether the particle, or the surrounding space is doing the moving, it is all relative, spacial, and temporal relativity laws apply regardless (equivalency principle). Gravity in an elevator is gravity through inertial motion, and obtains gravitational factors which are identical to gravity. This goes back to Einstein's elevator thought experiment, the equivalency principle.

In other words, the phase transformed particles of anti-matter in space becomes heavy and squashed short due to their velocity, then are pushed to inversion due to the fact that they are traveling faster than light. Mass amplification and relativity disallow this, with an additional gravitational penalty. The Nexus wave develops supergravity due to this phenomenon, which entangles to everything behind it, which it has created earlier in time.

This method of changing from anti-matter into matter (phase transition) avoids the energy annihilations which results when matter and anti-matter come in direct contact with each other. The matter phase transformational process. At the same time this is occurring, the particle is forced to decelerate very quickly (now in the spacial dimension) creating deceleration amplified inertia forces, in the matter state, while increasing its mass exponentially again. This phenomenon continues indefinitely with trillions of sub-atomic particles passing within the spherical Nexus wave front shell, phase transforming anti-matter into matter. Think of water transforming into steam. Laws of conservation of energy allows for this phenomenon to occur in nature.

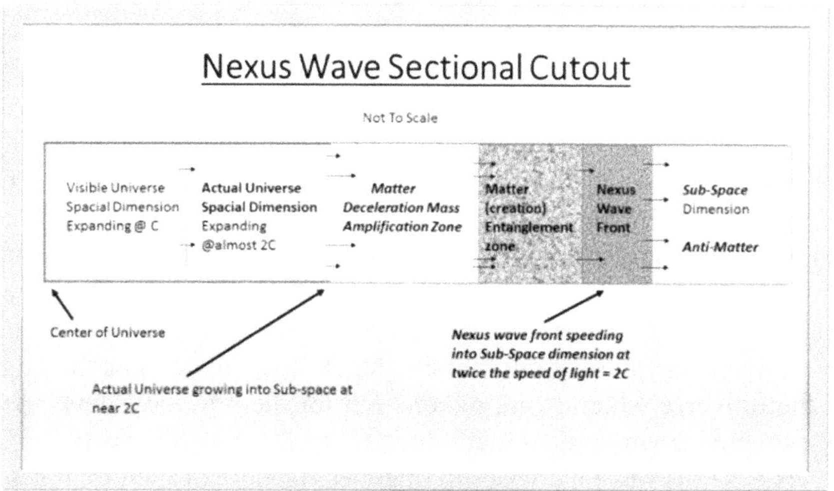

These mass amplified particles create super gravitational forces in the mass amplified state within the expanding Nexus wave sphere. This is occurring throughout the spherical Nexus bow shock wave, as it continues growing into the sub-spacial dimension while simultaneously expanding the actual spacial universe dimension, at the expense of the sub-spacial anti-matter universes domain.

Any anti-matter objects from the sub-spacial dimension are instantaneously phase transformed energy wise from the impact of the Nexus wave front. Whole planets and stars, black holes, are phase transformed into particles of matter, and gas, to start evolutionary life as matter based objects in the spacial dimension. Entire galaxies of matter would be being transformed in tacked, structure wise, after the phase-transformation effect overtakes them. The galactic matter would be in place to start the galactic, stars system and planetary evolution over again, in the spacial dimension, without the standard billion years of gravitational collection work required for evolution. It remains undetermined as to how much functional damage is incurred by means of Nexus wave phase transition to its victims in this discussion. Maybe we could think of the destruction encountered within the range of a supernova star to its solar system as a reference point of thought. We know the universe is a dangerous place to exist, with high energy events taking place, anywhere and any intervals.

The Nexus wave super gravity expedites spacial development of matter based astrophysical entities. Stars and black holes recoilless in less time that of natural evolution would require, as supergravity amplifies reconstruction of anti-matter converted matter, time requirements. Entangled super gravity with matter-based gravity entangle to quicken star and black hole reconstruction after nexus wave disruptions. This would also explain the short massive black hole evolution time frames that presently baffle astrophysics. This phenomenon explains how massive black holes exist near the edge of the universe which is not old enough for them to have developed by accepted cosmological methods.

The Nexus wave increases in thickness (spherical shell thickness) as it leads the spacial dimensional universal conversion expansion over time. The transforming matter experiencing beyond light speed physical relativity parameters, creating super mass amplified gravitational attraction for the time it is entangled within the Nexus wave system. The Nexus wave shell is approximately 188,000,000,000 light years in circumference at present, and millions of light years in spherical shell thickness, which creates a lot of mass amplified gravitational forces, in its wake (the actual universe) behind its movement.

This phenomenon creates a supergravity situation within itself (the actual universe), which entangles its supergravity to everything that it has created in the past (spacial dimension). This supergravity is entangled throughout the entire actual universe, which helped to create our spacial reality. The effects of its super gravity are still entangled with everything within the spacial dimension in which it created since the original big bang event 14 billion years ago. As it grows, it pulls on everything behind it, hence universal expansion, with acceleration, explained.

This Nexus wave, which creates supergravity, continues to grow at twice the speed of light and will continue to do so indefinitely into the sub-spacial dimension, due to the fact that there is no space in front of it, to slow it down.

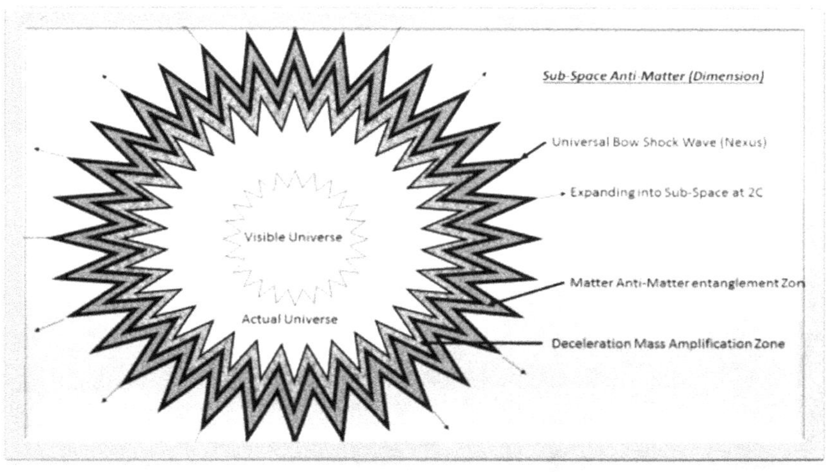

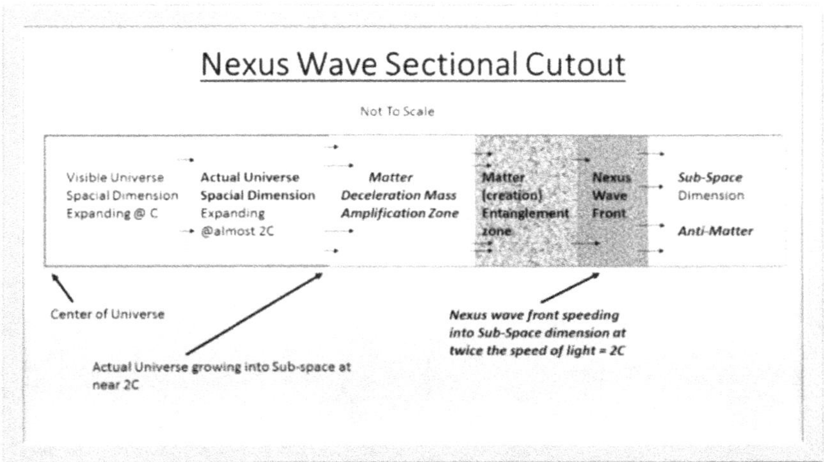

Original Sketches by author William Thomas

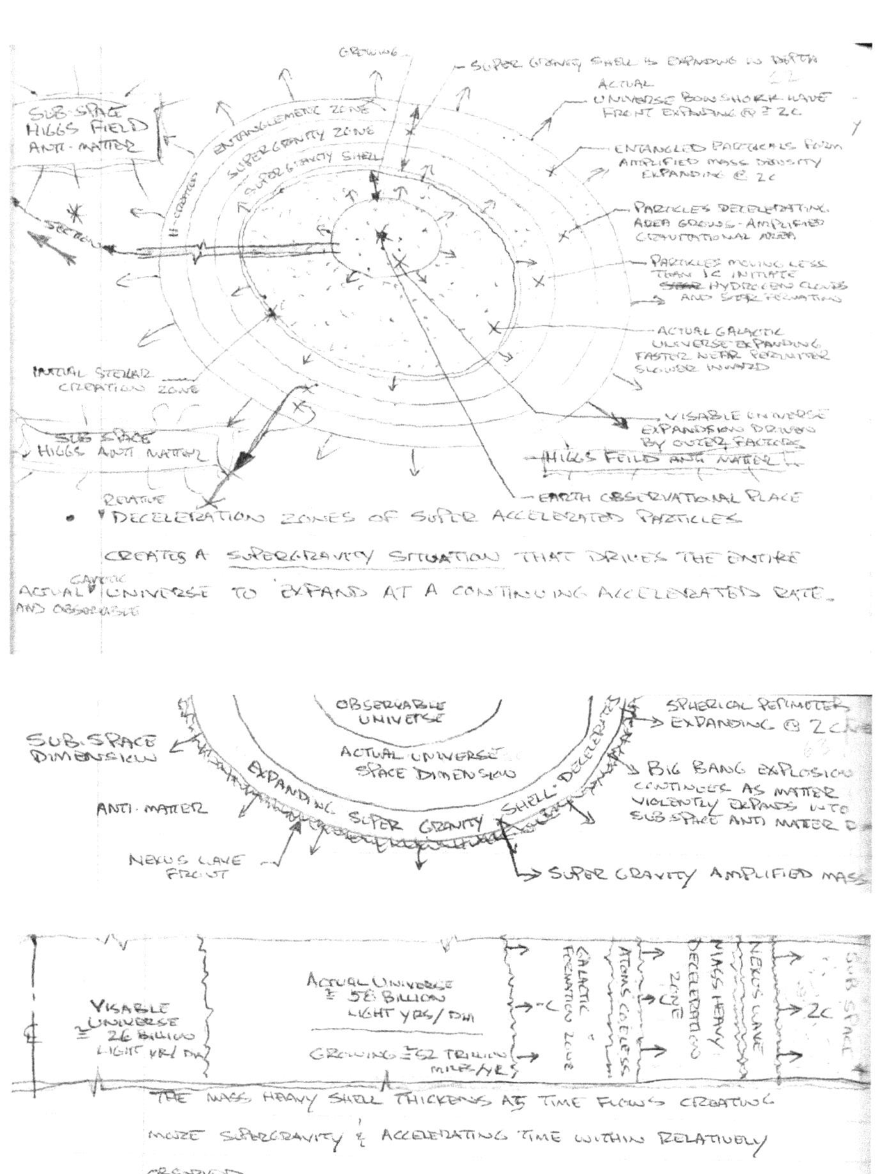

<u>Sectional view of Nexus wave front leading universal expansion</u>

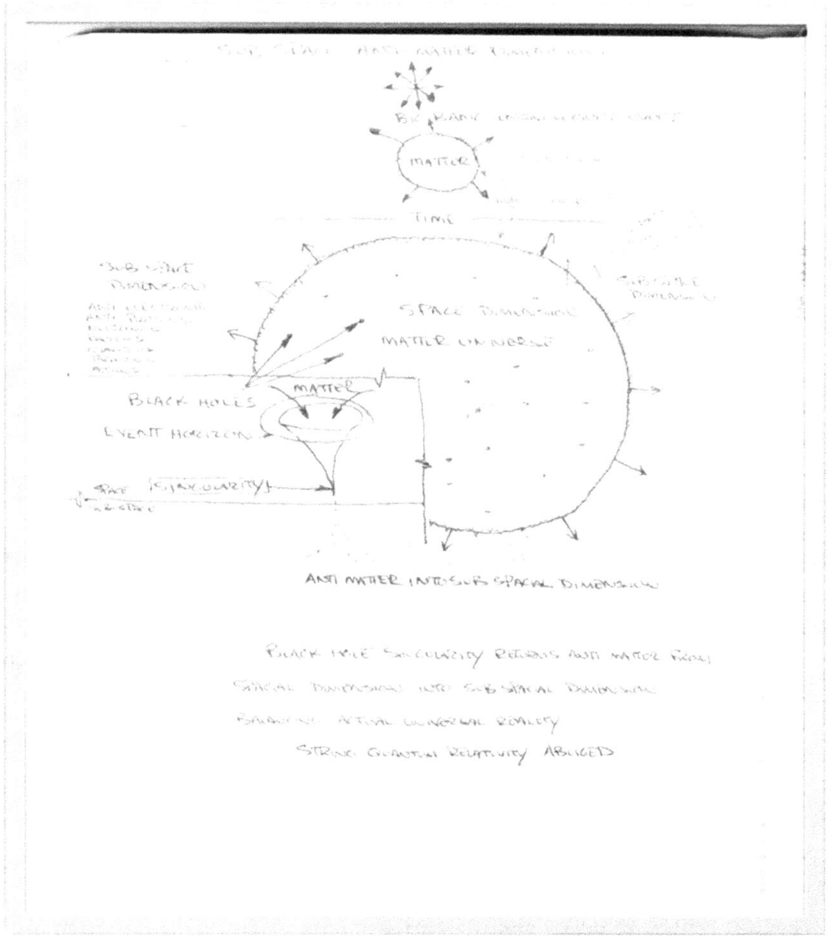

The sub-spacial dimension feeding anti-matter into the spacial dimension as converted matter by means of Nexus conversion, explains where all the matter in our universe came from without violating any laws of conservation. The sub-spacial dimension is feeding matter in to the spacial dimension by means of the Nexus wave front phase transition conversion phenomenon. It is written twice to ensure understanding.

There is simply too much matter in our universe to have come from a single point in space, or to have just appeared out of nowhere, from a mysterious energy source. That energy source would have to be trillions of time more powerful than the most powerful things we can observe today (super massive black holes)!

If there was that much matter in the initial big bang it should have formed a super massive black hole singularity, not an explosion. The only plausible explanation for an initial big bang explosion is to eliminate gravity as a physics factor. Science has put forth the premise that initially there were no physics, since there was no universe for physics to exist. If this were true, where did the matter or energy initially come from to initiate the big bang, and why did it explode as if gravity and space were in tacked physics' wise.

The sub-spacial phase transition to a spacial dimension by means of an energy incident, provides a plausible explanation of the universe we observe, with respect to the string theory discussion we are engaged within. Mathematics requires balance, matter and energy must balance, give and take. Laws of conservation of energy comply with the explanation of spacial dimension being created from a sub-spacial dimensional energy conversion incident. the phase transitioning of matter from sub-space into space, then returning it back through singularities, universe wide. Matter being created at the nexus wave front, from sub-space, then returned within singularities to sub-space equals a balanced equation.

The trillions of universal singularities which squash matter back into the sub-spacial dimension as anti-matter, explain how our complete reality balances its allocations of matter and anti-matter, also preserving the laws of conservation of energy. Matter is created at the in the Nexus wave front from sub-space, and returned through singularities to sub-space. The universal energy balance of reality.

Understanding the give and take of the spacial and sub-spacial dimensions, as space borrows matter, from sub-space and then later returns it back to sub-space, as the anti-matter, that it borrowed originally. The phase transition from one dimension to another may be destructive to the physical state of the matter and anti-matter; but reality is not concerned, it just balances its energy indefinitely. The universe is violent, it must be. Conservation of energy must be sustained regardless.

Think of the Yin and Yang balance in nature, give and take from old eastern philosophies. This give and take relationship allows both matter and anti-matter to exist, as well as space and sub-spacial dimensions, which give birth to our reality. The universe feeding itself from itself within, nothing is wasted. Reality is then greater than the sum of its parts, as all spacial dimensions entangle to give rise to a living consciousness which is able to experience the reality it has created.

Quantum entanglement of sub-atomic particles allows, life, consciousness, emotion, thought, imagination, communication, memory, spirituality, and the universe to sustain a working reality for both space and sub-spacial dimensions to exist, which uses matter and anti-matter to function, while abiding by relativity laws, energy conservation laws, Information paradox theory, uncertainty principles, entropy of a black hole theory, quantum mechanics, string theory, holographic principle, many world theory, to name a few.

Thought provocation is the goal of this discussion, and we still have a bit more to discuss. Open minded thinking provides the opportunity for new adventurous experiences. Dark matter may need a little light shinned upon it in the final chapter of this work.

Dark Matters

Science has been working to explain what dark matter, and dark energy are for some time now. It has long been known through telescopic observation that the universe is expanding at an accelerated rate, which defies logical reasoning. Earlier in this discussion we determined that ninety percent of the universe was just beyond our visual observational sight, due to time and relativity issues. With the visible universe being roughly fourteen billion years old, and light speed being what it is. Using basic mathematics, we can deduce that the visible universe is no more than fourteen billion miles in radius, or twenty-eight billion light years in spherical diameter.

Realizing that the universe is expanding into nothing, (sub-space) and relativity allows faster than light speed travel, when traveling in a non-spacial dimension. The gravitational forces at work (to cause the observed expansion) required to continuously expand the visible universe would require about ten times more mass in the universe, than we can detect. The obvious solution is that the universe is ten time larger that we can detect (due to relativity issues). We discussed this in the previous chapter.

We then do mathematics to speculate that there is ten times more mass than observable in the visible universe, the actual universe becomes twice the spherical diameter of the visible universe, thereby allowing ten times more galaxies in total estimation, to provide ten times more mass, to explain the galactic expansion we observe. The actual universe then becomes almost sixty billion light years in spherical diameter, give or take a billion. It also dictates that the actual universe is growing spherically at a rate of 24,000,000,000 miles a year in diameter.

That means that if we could observe the spacial dimensions universal growth from the sub-spacial dimension, we would see the

60 billion light year diameter sphere grow another 4 light years each year, or about 28,000,000 miles in spherical diameter every hour. It would not look like anything was growing, if we could look at it from a distance far enough away to actually observe the entire spherical universe due to its actual size. The Nexus wave front might look like a star if one could observe it from the sub-spacial dimension where it is invading, and growing into.

The Nexus bow shock wave front is moving into sub-space at twice the speed of light, meaning that our actual universe is growing at about four light years in diameter each year. That is equivalent to the distance from here to our nearest star system, Alfa Centari, our closest neighboring star system. The Nexus wave front crashes into sub-spacial dimension at close to 14,000,000 miles an hour, give or take. The reaction of anti-matter being transformed into matter at that speed must create quite a light show, if one were able to observe it.

That said we then deduce that the bow shock Nexus wave is moving at twice the speed of light into the sub-spacial dimension, even today. Nothing in front of it (space) to slow it down, or hinder its procession.

The supergravity created in the amplified inertial induced matter, by the Nexus wave front could be called the Dark Matter that scientists have been looking for in the past. Dark matter in this discussion is the cause of dark energy and is responsible for our universally accelerating expansion (galaxies moving away from each other with acceleration).

The Nexus wave created super-gravity can describe the expanding universe observations we've been making telescopically. The Dark Energy which is causing the galaxies to move away from each other in an accelerated manner, is caused by the supergravity, from Nexus wave, and by the trailing galaxies in the actual universe, following the Nexus wave, which are outside of our visible universe.

In other words, the amplified mass induced relatively heavy new matter in the bow shock Nexus wave pulls everything outward towards itself as it continues to move outward spherically from everything we know at twice the speed of light.

The galaxies in the outer perimeter of the universe gravitationally pull the inner (visible universal galaxies), outward with gravitational attraction. This is amplified by the entangled super-gravity created within the Nexus wave fronts wake. The Nexus wave pulls the outer galaxies outward, and this in turn pulls the inner galaxies outward. These phenomena create what science calls dark energy. Together these phenomena are what scientists are calling dark matter, which creates dark energy.

The super-gravity has residual effect which also entangles throughout the entire universe (all matter) creating mass in all sub-atomic particles.

The Nexus wave supergravity entangles back to everything in the actual universe, and helps to hold galaxies together. This super-gravity entangles (interacting with weak, and strong electromagnetic forces) through all sub-atomic matter in the spacial dimension to give mass to sub-atomic matter. It entangles into the galactic super massive black hole singularities, at the center of each galaxy. The galactic super massive black holes amplify the gravitational supergravity phenomenon, throughout the galaxies by means of entanglement.

Normal sized galactic black holes help to entangle the supergravity phenomenon throughout the entire galaxy, as they entangle with each other and their galactic center, and collectively throughout the entire universal web.

The super-gravity phenomena, and entangled event horizon information storage devices, create a continuum throughout reality which links sub-spacial dimensions with spacial dimensions, entangling all living consciousness by means of a super entanglement of information. Everything in reality is entangled, all dimensions, all consciousness, by means of entangled supergravity or electromagnetic energy (light). Strings create and maintain our reality. It's all relative.

The Supergravity pulls actual universal sub-atomic matter outward in all directions simultaneously acting like a magnetic soup that suspends the otherwise massless sub-atomic particles by means of static electromagnetic force, throughout the entire physical universe. This super gravity situation is being looked for presently by many, but as the Higgs boson field or the god particle, which is providing difficult to verify, as well as expensive to look for and research into.

Super gravity is plausible, inexpensive to utilize, and verifiable through logical deduction and observation. Akums' razor, relativity and quantum physics concur. Supergravity's (Nexus wave) mass inertia amplified deceleration shell converts phase transitioned matter into a gravitationally entangling subatomic matter field, causing mass in all sub-atomic matter by means of its very existence. The quantum entanglement of super-gravity throughout the universe causes mass in sub-atomic particles.

The big bang bow shock wave front called the Nexus wave, is moving at twice the speed of light which creates an enigmatic temporal reality. The outer galaxies pull the inner galaxies outward words towards the Nexus wave, the Nexus wave pulls the outer galaxies outward words towards itself as it expands into sub-space.

Newly phase-transformed anti-matter into matter from Nexus wave front, transformation of stars, and planets leaves them mostly in tacked, but as if they were in a train wreck. The matter from the newly transformed object requires much less time to reinitiate planetary and stellar maturity. The entangled supergravity from the retreating Nexus wave (gone by) is still very strong, and simplifies amplified gravitational developmental mass recovery efforts. It takes less time to make planets and stars than we originally estimated due to supergravity, nearer to the actual universe perimeter.

This entangled supergravity action accelerates new star, and planet formation. The super gravity accelerates gravitational attractions in galactic development as well as galactic strand, and galactic filament development (*the web of galaxies in the universe when observed, appears to look like a brain scan, with trillions neuron connections*). It accelerates living consciousness evolution by means of communication, imagination, technology, etc. Human technology advances by means of imagination, to creation, as fast as possible. Imagination is retrieved through sub-spacial dimensions as entangled communicational by products of shared information throughout reality.

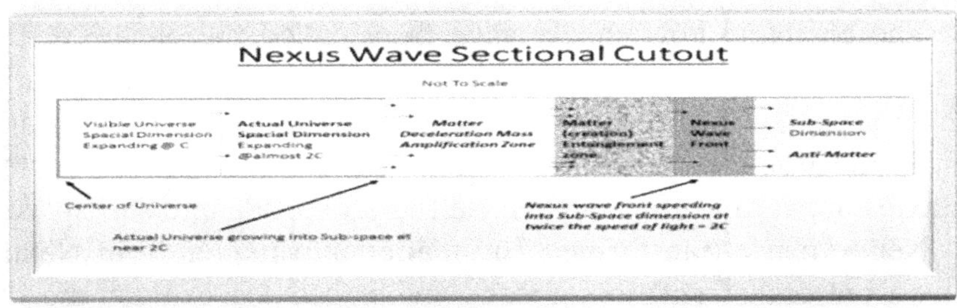

Nexus Wave Sectional Cutout
Not To Scale
Visible Universe Spacial Dimension Expanding @ C
Actual Universe Spacial Dimension Expanding @almost 2C
Matter Deceleration Mass Amplification Zone
Matter (creation) Entanglement Zone
Nexus Wave Front
Sub-Space Dimension
Anti-Matter
Center of Universe
Actual Universe growing into Sub-space at near 2C
Nexus wave front speeding into Sub-Space dimension at twice the speed of light = 2C

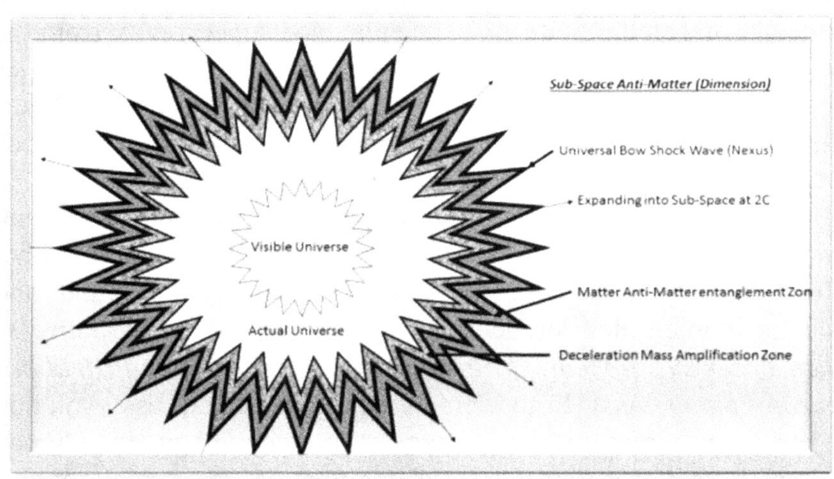

Sub-Space Anti-Matter (Dimension)
Universal Bow Shock Wave (Nexus)
Expanding into Sub-Space at 2C
Visible Universe
Matter Anti-Matter entanglement Zon
Actual Universe
Deceleration Mass Amplification Zone

Temporal Relativity

Things get a little bit weird when we attempt to get a handle on time, near the Nexus wave front perimeter due to relativity (temporal) issues. Let's start by imagining that we are riding in the Nexus wave (surfing it) in our galaxy class space ship as it travels into sub-space at twice the speed of light.

It would appear to us that we were traveling into a dark void of nothing, assuming we could see through the Nexus phenomenon visually. Time paradox is created from excessive our velocity, moving beyond our familiar present into the unknown. At twice light speed relativity compressed our space ship, and bodies into a flat material state, as it the inverts us inside out, again into a darkness void, where our reality is changed. If that wasn't enough, we have also attained infinite mass in our inverted states of being. Possibly transforming into the sub-spacial dimension of imagination and anti-matter due to our adventurous space ride at the edge of reality. Imagination allows this look into the theoretical astrophysical phenomena beyond the universes outer perimeter.

Let's then imagine that we were still riding in the Nexus wave, still in our galaxy class space ship while we were looking outward into the sub-spacial dimension. What is it you think; we would see from that perspective? Imagine what it might look like, remember that your imagination entangles into the sub-spacial dimensions as a natural phenomenon of reality. What picture in the many world's theory reality does your mind create in this situation? Is it different than my picture, it must be, due to perspective observational experiences of different individuals.

If we looked back from that which we came, from the window of our galaxy class space ship, what would we see while moving at twice the speed of light? Would it seem from that perspective that we were in a lightning flash of some sort, since the light coming from the actual universe would not be able to keep up with us, and there would be no light in front of us, in the sub-spacial dimension of anti-matter? We would be surfing in darkness, essentially being nowhere! Would Nexus create light energy as it transformed anti-matter sub-space into material in space? Imagination can create a vision of this, but our reality cannot, with respect to relativity, of distance and technology limitations.

All around us would be phase transitioned sub-atomic particles transforming into infinitely heavy mass induced states of matter, creating an energetic gravitational static charge which would likely destroy us. It might be like an inverted black hole as we were ridding inside the bow shock wave front of Nexus. It might also be like riding inside of a bolt of lightning. What do you think it would be like?

Let's now imagine that we are in our galaxy class space ship observing the universe from a place close to the outer edge of the actual universe, but far enough inward from the outer perimeter to not be destroyed by the Nexus wave. When we looked towards the Nexus wave we would only see blackness, due to the velocity of the wave. It would be moving away from us at speeds faster than light, so we would not be able to see it, and no stars would have had time to form yet between us and it. It would appear like a black hole, or giant black void in front of the space ship.

If we then turned back, to look towards the interior of the actual universe from our space ship, we would perceive the rest of the universe shrinking away from us, due to us moving outward in an accelerating velocity from the pull of the Nexus wave's super gravity. If we were close enough to the Nexus wave, and traveling faster than light, we would only see darkness looking back, and possibly forward also, depending on the relative speed differences between all three, the ship, Nexus, and the actual universe.

From earths perspective the universe appears to be expanding at an accelerating velocity, yet from the outskirts of the same universe, the universe appears to be shrinking when looking inward at it.

Relativity is relative to the observational perspective of the observer. There is no absolute time in this universe thanks to the relativity laws, and their restrictions. Einstein showed us this, and our technological atomic clocks then proved it. Time is not the same on one star to the next star for the same observer, due to time, relativity, and spacial dimensional parameters.

Temporal dimensional flexibility, observational perspectives in relativity, are more enigmatic when thought about on this level. Time and observation become confusion and unrealistic when observed from certain perspectives in the outer regions of the physical universe in certain thought experiments. If you could look at the expanding universe from outside of its perimeter, while existing in the sub-space dimension in which it is growing into, the spherical shell could appear to be shrinking to you, due to its velocity, relative to your observation. Moving so much faster than light it could appear to move back in time. The laws of temporal relativity in sub-space may differ from our same laws in the spacial dimension. Since the Nexus wave is moving into sub-space at twice the speed of light, we can deduce that temporal relativity follows different equational aspects in sub-space, than in our spacial dimension.

Nexus wave is moving at twice the speed of light in the spacial dimensional perspective, and it would be traveling through relative time at factors of multitude far different from our own clocks allow. From that point of view, or even from inside the universal sphere, no one could correctly observe those temporal parameters at the edge of reality, due to the relativity factors of observable velocity that it are just beyond human capacity in our understanding of science in the sub-spacial dimension.

Imagine you could instantaneously place yourself and the galaxy class space ship at about one hundred and sixty million light years from earth. Imagine you have a telescope that can see events on the surface of earth, from that distance. You would then be able to watch dinosaurs roaming the earth, in prehistoric times. Move the space ship to about a hundred light years from earth and you would be able to watch world war 1 occurring, in real time. Now imagine how a race of intelligent extraterrestrials would think of us if they were watching in on our earthly stage, with such a telescope. Let's hope they would happen to do so while humans were in a period of good behaviors. What would they think of us?

When scientist look deep into the universe with technological telescopes, they may actually be looking at the younger parts of the universe, instead of older parts. The galaxies nearer to the edge of the actual universe are younger than our galaxy, due to the fact that they have been born into the spacial dimension more recently than our own Milky Way galaxy. The outer galaxies are close to the edge of the universe where it is expanding into the sub-spacial dimension as we discuss these topics. Time on a wrist watch is not of much use to cosmological time keeping efforts with respect to Einstein's relativity science. It is fun to use our living consciousness to think about such things as the individual's imagination creates virtual realities within our multi dimension dimensional sub-spacial sentient selves.

I hope you enjoyed the discussions, and thank you for partaking in it with me. Have a great day, and more enjoyable experiences in this reality as time marches past you.

www.ingramcontent.com/pod-product-compliance
Lightning Source LLC
Chambersburg PA
CBHW071015180726
48291CB00004B/1475